CW01501384

Val Whitehouse © 2024

Printed in the UK

First Printing: 2024

Chapter 1

There's nothing special about my village, except perhaps the slight mystery surrounding its name: Middle Pidding. You see, there isn't a Lower Pidding or an Upper Pidding. Your guess is as good as mine as to where they disappeared to, if they ever existed. My husband-who-thinks-he's-so-clever has the theory that the cartographers mis-spelt Pidding so many times that they hastened to re-name the others to save embarrassment. He has a point – you try typing PIDDING and I'll bet you automatically hit that L after the double D. Anyway, it's an ordinary village. We have a church with a wounded steeple, hit by a myopic rear gunner in WW2; a pub called We Anchor in Hope, even though we are nowhere near the sea; a church hall which is the public hub of the community and two coffee shops which are the private hubs; little shops ranging from boutiques and hairdressers for those who still care about their own appearances to DIY and hardware emporiums for those who have transferred that care into their houses. There's a small supermarket, as well as butchers and bakers and candlestick makers. A normal village.

You will be wondering who I am. Well, you remember that I told you there were two coffee shops? I own one of them. I specialise in gorgeous cakes, though I do say it myself, and I call my shop The Cake Mutiny. Sorry, it was my husband's idea and as he was putting up half the money I thought it wise to concur. I can't be bothered with all that barista stuff so I just serve good instant. The other coffee establishment has a gleaming machine that puffs and pants and finally delivers a frothy concoction that some prefer – but their cakes are hideous. So you pays your money and you takes your choice – and I'm happy to say that this village tends to prefer a macaroon to a macchiato.

My name is the same as my grandmother's: Jennifer Nora Enid Dottinger. My father always called me Jenny Anydots, and you can see why, can't you? (Jenny N.E. Dottinger? See?) He added that T.S.Eliot met my grandmother once, but I couldn't see any connection there – however, it pleased him, so there you are. My husband has since enlightened me. I was overjoyed to change the Dottinger bit when I got married to Tom Brandon. He's in insurance, by the way, and has a little office above my shop. It makes feeding him very easy, although he has become decidedly less svelte over the years. More fuzzy svelte!

2

Tom says that running a coffee shop is rather like being a bartender serving needy customers. "Set 'em up, Joe" and then they proceed to tell you their life story. You'd be surprised at the number of secrets, guilty and otherwise, that get leaked to me. Either that, or I just happen to overhear whispered conversations that I can fit together like a jigsaw: one little fact here that meshes nicely with another one there. That's how I came to work out who the **murderer** was. Oh, wait a minute. I haven't told you about that, have I? Silly me, that was the whole point of my writing this book! I'll start at the beginning and you can work it out as I go along.

Chapter 2

Middle Pidding puts on a pantomime every year, and very good it is, too. The Dramatic Society has been going for yonks and they rehearse and perform in the ubiquitous Village Hall. They are always directed by Greatorex Manston who is a local entrepreneur and property developer. Greaty, as we all call him, puts his heart and soul into the panto. He's a handsome chap – tall, blonde, blue-eyed and extremely eligible. No-one is quite sure how he's evaded marriage for so long (he's in his late thirties, you see) and certain cynical people have intimated that he's gay, but as they usually said that after he'd turned them down for a part, I'm taking it with a pinch of the proverbial condiment. He dresses beautifully and wears an exotic after-shave that sends the senses reeling (don't tell Tom I said that!) but I'm a good judge of these things and I think he's as straight as a pie. Certainly, his P.A. agrees with me and she sees his personal diary and everything. I don't think he could hide anything from her. Judging by the way her eyes follow him around with that certain look in them, I think she'd love to put him to the test, if you see what I mean. She's called

Goody Gofer, which is a very appropriate surname because she rushes around at his peck and call. You'd think they would see enough of each other at work every day, but Goody is also his Stage Manager. She'd live in his pocket if she could but he never seems to view her as anything but an assistant. Poor Goody. There's none so blind as those who will not pee.

This year's panto is 'Cinderella' and they started rehearsing months ago. The first casting meeting happened in The Cake Mutiny one Saturday…

"Cinders is obviously the main problem. Leela will expect to be cast," says Greaty with a theatrical sigh.

"She's fifty if she's a day," exclaims Jack, the Technical Director.

"I know, I know. But she's a founder member of the Society and she's always played the lead."

Goody stirs her coffee thoughtfully. "Do you think we could persuade her that the Fairy Godmother is actually the main character so that she'd want to play that?"

"Not unless we change the title of the panto," replies Greaty. "Would you like to be the one to tell her?"

"Not Pygmalion likely. I'd never be able to go into her flower shop again – not unless I wanted wilted blooms and half-dead plants from then on. You're the only one who could charm her into believing it. You could do it, you know," she says, with doe eyes and batting eyelashes.

"Greaty could persuade her to be the back end of the 'orse, if you ask me," says Jack. "Talk about fridges and eskimos."

"I think you'll find that it's Inuits nowadays, Jack," corrects Greaty.

"I'll never know 'ow you managed to get me to build your first set all those years ago. I ended up thinking you was doing me a favour by 'aving me on the team!"

"That was 'Dick Whittington', wasn't it? "Twelve o'clock and not a sign of Dick!" Oh, we love those double entendres, don't we? So English! What a happy production that was," says Greatorex, preening.

"Leela 'ad a fine figure then. Wonderful Principal Boy. But there's been a lot of gin under the bridge since then. No matter 'ow many soft filters I put into her spotlight, I can't take twenty-five years off 'er age."

"Oh dear. I don't think there's any way round it. She'll have to be Cinderella. We can only hope that our faithful audience will look with rose-coloured spectacles," says Goody, tucking her neat legs further under the table and slightly nearer to Greaty's.

"So that leaves Bunty Beaufort and Mimi Merry to slog it out for Fairy Godmother and Wicked Stepmother at the auditions. By the way, are those theatrical names or their real ones?" asks Greaty.

"Real, I think. Nicely alliterative, aren't they? Always looks good on the programme. I'd suggest Mimi as the Fairy Godmother. She's got more of a twinkle than Bunty," says Goody.

"Yes. We could give her 'Nobody Loves a Fairy When She's Forty' to sing in the first Act," agrees Greaty.

"Even though she'll never see forty again?" queries Jack.

"Especially so. That means Bunty for the Wicked Stepmother. Now she's only working part-time she'll have more leisure in which to learn her lines."

"What about the Ugly Sisters?" queries Goody.

"Bertram as one. Maybe Robbie Slack for the other?" suggests Greaty.

"Blimey. Robbie won't like that. Bertram working in Robbie's pub has put Robbie right off 'im. Robbie reckons he's been fiddling the till," laughs Jack. "But you didn't 'ear that from me, all right?" he adds hastily.

"We'll have to use the horse costume this year. Wendy spent ages making it two years ago and was fuming that we didn't put it into 'Sleeping Beauty' last year," warns Goody, managing to slide her dainty little shoes next to Greaty's brogues under the table.

"Oh. We'll work it into the script somehow. It can pull the golden coach."

"What golden coach?" erupts Jack. "No-one mentioned a ruddy golden coach before."

"But Jack, dear, everyone knows that Cinders gets transported to the ball in a golden…" starts Goody gently.

"No way. I can't be expected to build a ruddy coach, gold or otherwise!"

"Don't fret, Jack. It will be a suggestion off in the wings," Greaty says soothingly. "No need for anyone to see the actual coach."

"All right," agrees a mollified Jack. "Back to the 'orse, then. You could get a married couple to be inside it to save any embarrassment. Titty and Tony Cropper would do. Put Tony at the back so 'e can nuzzle up to Titty's bum."

"Good idea. Though I really think we should use her proper name: Titania. It sounds so much more theatrical."

"Sounds bleedin pretentious to me."

"What about the Handsome Prince?" asks Greaty, moving on.

"Got to be our lovely new member, Chris," replies Goody emphatically.

"But he's black!" yelps Jack.

"Now, now. Pantomimes are already gender-blind, so there's no reason why they can't be colour-blind as well. He's a gorgeous looking chap. Mind you, he'll show up Leela's age. Will the audience accept them as a young couple?" worries Greaty.

"It's panto. They'll accept anything. Though I suppose we could make him Buttons instead?" muses Goody, still luxuriating in the thought of the handsome Chris as anything at all.

"No, Buttons has got to be Freddy. He's got such a cheeky way of charming all the old biddies. Chris will have to be the Prince," says Greaty decidedly.

"We'll 'ave to call 'im the "Black Prince!""

"That's it, then. We'll call an audition for next week and let them all think we haven't made our minds up even though we have. So this is just between ourselves until then – no leaking to anyone."

They pledge their words on keeping silent about their conversation, and Greatorex turns to look at the array of splendid cakes on the counter.

"Jenny! Can we have some of your wonderful Victoria Sponge over here? And another coffee. Thank you, darling."

They must have thought I was deaf. Keeping it just between themselves, indeed. But that's what happens in here: I blend into the background and hear everything! So I know the cast long before anyone else. There it is, done and dustbinned.

Chapter 3

Have I confused you? I've thrown quite a lot of names at you so perhaps I'd better fill you in on a bit of background. First of all, there's Leela Davies, the one who's got to be Cinderella. She's got a flair for colour and window dressing so her flower shop is a picture. She knows it, too. She likes to tell everyone that she was trained at Harrods, but I know for a fact that she only had a Saturday job there when she was a teenager. To hear her talk, you'd think she was a particular favourite of Mr Fayed himself. She certainly thinks she's a cut above anyone else in the village. I call her the Barbara Cartland of Middle Pidding so that should give you a fair picture of what she looks like. She's well-preserved and she must spend her old man's money with gay abandon because she's always wearing new clothes and having 'treatments' in London. They must use a lot of pollyfiller, that's all I can say. Or what's that stuff called that freezes out the wrinkles? Botox? She must have shares in that. After that description you may be surprised to hear that I quite like her. She's not one of those weight-wary women who won't touch cake. No, she's a cream cake fan and she swears that her old feller likes a bit to get hold of in a woman. Maybe he does, because they always look happy enough together. She often comes in here for her lunch – I do lovely sandwiches as well as cakes – so we've had some great chats setting the world to fights.

She does have a rival or two in the Dramatic Society. First of all, there's Mimi Merry, who'll be playing the Fairy Godmother. She's about the same age as Leela but much more flashy. Christmas trees come to mind. Give her a costume and she'll be sewing sequins on by the end of the first rehearsal. Her humour is a bit ribald at times but she's good company. She's got a sharp tongue and you don't want to get on the wrong side of her but we hit it off. You'd never believe that she was our District Nurse but you'll see her buzzing around the village in her mini bringing solace to the sick. I love it when she comes into the café when she's got some free time in her rounds. What a gossip! I always have a laugh with her and you know what they say about the best medicine. She's a good one to have around in a crisis, too, because she's very practical and level-headed when she needs to be. I'm very glad she was there when we discovered the **murder**!

I'd better toss another character into the pot, and that's Bunty Beaufort. She's also one of the founder members. She's in her late fifties and doesn't mind your knowing it. She's mutton dressed as mutton. Having said that, she's quite pleasant to look at: I don't mean to suggest that she's an ugly old bag. She dresses smartly but plainly. She's the local pharmacist so I suppose she has to appear well turned out. You wouldn't want to have your medicines mixed by a scruff. We all thought she'd take early retirement and go on a world cruise but she keeps hanging on. She's just a part-timer now but the job carries a lot of importance and I don't think she's quite ready to let that go. She'll make a good Wicked Stepmother. She can be very haughty and aloof if she wants. Come to think of it, she's a stepmother in real life, though those kids are now grown up and moved away. But she'll be able to give the part some reality. What am I talking about? Panto is about as far from reality as you can get!

Tony and Titania Cropper will be the Horse (or the 'orse, as Jack would say). They're a strange couple. They took over the Off Licence a few years ago when the bloke who used to own it died unsurprisingly of liver failure. Tony's a bit of a control freak and he keeps a close eye on Titty, as we call her. She suffers from migraines, which I often think she uses as an excuse to get away from her husband for a day or two. If I was married to him, I'd want time off in a darkened room too. She's quite a pretty little thing, with a Shirley Temple look about her when she dimples up in a smile. He's a miserable sod, always complaining about something. Shirley and Surly, you might say. Their rival establishment for alcoholic beverages is the pub, which is run by Robbie Slack. He's a Jack-the-Lad who's never really settled down, though his wife Alice does her best to keep him reined in. They make the pub a friendly place to get a drink and a snack. His main barman is Bertram Taylor. I used to think they were a good pairing but I've started to notice a bit of friction between them. Making them the Ugly Sisters may help to bond them back together or it may fracture them completely. Time will yell. Watch this space!

I could go through the whole village like this but you'd be throwing the book across the room if I did. I think the best thing to do is to show you what the first rehearsal was like. You'll pick up much more about people that way. By the way, I'm the Prompt, so I'm your reliable witness who watches everything without having to take too much part in the proceedings. You may be wondering why the Prompt was needed at all at a first rehearsal, but Greatorex always wants the Prompt there from day one. He says that a performance isn't just about the words but also about the pauses. Mimi used to call him Pinter behind his back till he cottoned on to it and told her off. Anyway, he insists that every pause has to be carefully plotted into the Prompt copy. He's right, too. We had an inexperienced Prompt a few years ago who kept calling out the next line in the middle of a laughter break. It's a wonder she didn't get murdered, I can tell you! But she lived to tell the kale. Mind you, she never did another play with us. Whenever she prompted anyone, they always told her afterwards that they hadn't needed it (even though they had) and she lost all her confidence. It's a hard job being the Prompt. You have to be very sure before you give a line, but you mustn't leave it too long so there's an embarrassing gap. It needs finesse. That poor kid just didn't have the knack and I think if she'd prompted another play she'd have been the **murder** victim!

Chapter 4

Greatorex, Goody and Jack arrive together at the Village Hall for the first rehearsal, armed with folders, spare scripts and notebooks. Goody, experienced S.M. that she is, always has a stock of pencils for people to mark up their scripts. You'd have thought everyone would bring their own, but you'd be wrong. The cries of 'Oh, I'll remember that move, darling. No need to write it down' can never be trusted. Greaty makes sure everyone makes a note straight away. It causes some problems because moves inevitably get changed as rehearsals proceed, and someone always forgets their glasses and writes instructions in the wrong place, but on the whole it's the best method. Goody buys a stock of nice little pencils that have an eraser on the end, bless her. Greaty has his own script, of course, with all his planned moves written down; Goody marks her copy as we proceed; and I mark mine. If ever there's a dispute about a move (and there always is) then Goody gets called on to arbitrate and I'm there as final backstop. We run a tight shit.

At about five to seven, everyone, including me, starts arriving. I always sit with Greaty and Goody

– ooh, I've just thought – the Great and the Good! Sorry, that just popped into my head. There are chairs ranged round in a circle for everyone just for the initial chat but we'll clear them to the side once we get going properly. Titania and Tony arrive together, naturally, but they're obviously mid quarrel as usual.

"I told you not to drink the soup too quickly, Tony. It's not my fault if you burnt your tongue."

"Why did you have to do a hot meal tonight? A bit of forward planning wouldn't go amiss."

"If I'd done a cold dinner you wouldn't have liked that, either. There's no pleasing you."

You see what I mean. I bet when they're in that horse costume there'll be a bit of bum-biting going on. Getting the bit between his teeth! I'm not sure how long they've been in padlock – sorry, wedlock – but they aren't much of an advert for wedded bliss. They used to be Bridge partners, too, but that ended a couple of years back and the whole Bridge Club sighed with relief when Tony didn't re-join. Perhaps he went one no trump too many. Titania does much better without him. I think she partners Bertram now.

Leela and Bunty rush in together, anxious not to be late. Leela is never tardy to rehearsals, but I think that's mainly because she doesn't want people to have time to talk about her before she arrives.

"Hello, darlings. Isn't it grand to be together again!" she says.

"We all see each other every day, Leela dear. You sound as if we've been apart since the last play," huffs Bunty.

"Yes, darling, but that's as ordinary people and this is as thespians. There's a huge difference."

Robbie is the next to arrive, explaining to everyone that he had to wait for the hired help to arrive at the pub before he could leave. He doesn't like the fact that Bertram is in the panto, because having both of them absent from the pub means he has to pay out for another barperson to help Alice cope. When Bertram arrives just after him, he gives him a poisonous glare. If looks could kill and all that. Oh dear, perhaps I shouldn't have said that considering later events…

"I'm afraid Chris and Freddy can't be with us tonight," says Greaty, "so Jenny will read in the Prince and Buttons."

"I bet they're up to no good together!" laughs Bertram. "They're as camp as tent pegs, both of them!"

"That's enough of that, Bertram. We don't talk about the cast's personal lives behind their backs."

"He said spinelessly," says Robbie, digging Bertram in the ribs.

I should explain. Robbie and Bertram have this word competition going between them. They try to come up with adjectives which are puns around the previous sentence – like just now, we had 'behind their backs' followed by 'spinelessly'. Sometimes they're really funny, but usually they're just too contrived. If anyone laughs out loud, that's a feather in the crap of whoever came up with it. There aren't many laughs, I can tell you, but there is the occasional smile.

"We're just waiting for Mimi, then we can begin."

"I did tell her it was a seven o'clock start," says Goody, getting a bit flustered. She can't bear the thought of failing in front of Greaty.

At that moment, in rushes Mimi.

"Sorry, folks. Something came up. And with my old man, if something comes up, you can't ignore it," she laughs suggestively.

"All right, so now we're all here. Oh, I told Wendy she needn't come tonight as we won't be discussing costumes for a couple of weeks. First of all, welcome to everyone. Goody has typed up the full cast list, so I'll just give you a minute to look at it and absorb the host of talent that we have at our disposal. Goody, dear, would you mind handing it out? I'll post it on the board as well so the village can get excited about it. We've only got six months to rehearse, so we want to take every opportunity to publicise ourselves."

"I'd hoped that Wendy would be here tonight," pouts Mimi. "I've got a couple of ideas for my cossie that I wanted to go over with her. They're going to need a lot of sewing so she'll have to start straight away."

"Are we talking sequins, dear?" asks Leela innocently.

"Just a smattering, darling," is the reply. "I am a Fairy, after all."

"I thought that only applied to Freddy," smirks Bertram.

I pin the cast list to the notice board while they all
check that I've spelt their names right. You'll want
to see the cast list, too, just so you can refer to it
whenever you're confused. Here it is:

Director	**Greatorex Manston**
S.M.	**Goody Gofer**
Set/Lights	**Jack Gofer**
Wardrobe	**Wendy Cotton**
Prompt	**Jenny Brandon**
Cinderella	**Leela Davies**
Prince	**Chris Monk**
Stepmother	**Bunty Beaufort**
Ugly Sisters	**Robbie Slack** **and** **Bertram Taylor**
Buttons	**Freddy Campton**
Fairy Godmother	**Mimi Merry**
Horse	**Tony and Titania Cropper**

Don't worry, you'll soon have them imprinted on your memory, especially when we get to the **murder**! Hold on a little bit longer. Patience is a verbal.

"You've all had the script for a few days now," Greaty continues. "Is everyone happy?"

"I've always pictured Cinderella coming down a grand staircase at the Ball. Any problem with that, Jack?" asks Leela cheekily.

Jack is gritting his teeth whilst trying to smile. He doesn't quite manage it. Goody steps in before her brother says something he may regret. (Did I tell you they were brother and sister? Sorry, I meant to.) She's always stepping in to save him: Big Sis looking after Little Bro. She also knows that Leela loves to wind people up and suggesting something virtually impossible on their meagre stage is a grand way to get to Jack. Naughty Leela!

"Don't fret, Leela. Jack has never failed us yet."

"Just saying. I have to picture the set before I can start to learn my words. We've only got six months, you know."

"It's the bloody coach I'm worried about," moans Tony. "Me and Titty will be the mugginses dragging it on and off."

"Hold your horses," puns Greaty. "It will all be done by suggestion and sleight of hand."

"He said deceptively," says Robbie.

"I must say I was surprised to see that the Wicked Stepmother wasn't being played by a man," says Mimi. "I thought she was usually a drag act, along with the Ugly Sisters, but I suppose Bunty is the next best thing. Oh my, I didn't mean that to come out quite like that!" she adds, hoping to stir up a bit of trouble. "I meant that Bunty was definitely the best thing. A bit of make-up works wonders. I was just a bit surprised."

Greaty rushes in as quickly as he can. The last thing he wants is for Bunty to storm off thinking she's been chosen because she's ugly in real life.

"It requires enormous acting talent to portray the conceited meanness of the Stepmother. Enormous talent. I knew dear Bunty could project ugliness and conceit, just the opposite of herself."

"Absolutely," agrees Mimi, beaming slyly.

"And I don't think the Stepmother is usually a drag act. I've never seen it done like that," adds Goody.

"Maybe I'm thinking of Widow Twanky," muses Mimi, revelling in the storm she almost caused.

"While we're on the subject of casting, I'm not sure I'm right for one of the Ugly Sisters. There's my moustache for a start. I'm not shaving it off," asserts Bertram.

"That's going to be one of our running jokes, Bertram. It will be hilarious," says Greaty.

"Yes, but couldn't I be Buttons and let Freddy be an Ugly Sis?"

"Freddy's far too camp. He'll be a lovely cheeky Buttons, but the whole point of a panto dame is that he's really masculine."

"No-one could doubt your virility, darling," says Mimi, with just enough flirtatiousness to embarrass Bertram.

"I think Greaty's done a wonderful job on the casting," says Titania supportively. "I'm not complaining about being the front end of the horse, am I?"

"No, dear. After all, you could have been a cow," quips Mimi.

"She said moooodily," says Robbie.

"If we'd been doing 'Jack and the Beanstalk', I mean," explains Mimi.

"Why don't we trot through the first act and see how it goes?" says Greaty. "It usually falls into place when we start to feel our characters."

I'm not going to bore you with the panto script. It was just what you'd expect. There are lots of no-she-isn't/yes-she-ises, several look-behind-yous, dames in frilly pantaloons doing prat falls, magical transformations behind sparkly curtains and a saccharine happy ending. There, I've saved you the pain of having to listen to them fluffing their way through it. I hope I've given you a feeling for some of the emotions on and under the surface. There are layers: there's how the people really are overlaid by the people they want you to think they are overlaid by the character they play in the production. It's a puzzling mixture sometimes. When the **murder** actually happens, they'll all emerge in their true colours, I suppose. All will be reviled.

Chapter 5

I'm going to move you on a few months now. The panto is well into rehearsals and the undercurrents are rising to the surface a bit more. Let me recall for you a typical day in the coffee shop. Imagine me flitting around serving while listening in to all sorts of titbits. See what you can pick up by way of clues to a possible **murder**. My first customers are Goody and Titty. They're good friends and they try to have breakfast here together several times a week. They think they're whispering but Titty's as deaf as a toast in one ear (we think Tony may have slapped her around a bit and left his indelible mark on her earoles) and Goody thinks if she sits with her back to me I won't hear her. They always have the same thing, white coffee with croissants and jam, and they then twitter their way to the last crumbs before leaving.

"Is Greaty pleased with the rehearsals so far, Goody?" asks Titty, licking my home-made apricot jam off her fingers.

"He's a bit worried about people learning their words – as usual. Bunty is worse than ever this year. Last night she came out with something that was in last year's panto, which threw everyone. I'm sure there's something on her mind."

"She's never got over that incident last February when old Mr Higgins died. She was the full-time and only pharmacist back then. His family made such a fuss about him having the wrong dose of medicine. Do you think it might still be on her mind?"

"Oh, Titania, I hope not. The Coroner exonerated her completely. Personally, I think his family gave him a double dose and his old ticker couldn't take it. I'm not saying it was on purpose, mind, but I think they accused Bunty just to draw attention away from themselves."

"You're probably right, but I heard Bertam say the Higginses were advising people to go over to Walmsley Ayrton to get their prescriptions filled."

"That's mean. I do hope Bunty hasn't heard that. If she has, I wouldn't blame her for being distracted. Should I tell Greaty?"

"I wouldn't. It's still three months till the panto. She's a trouper, she'll pull herself together," says Titty.

"I just don't want dear Greaty to criticise her too much if she's struggling with personal problems. What would we do if she walked out?"

"It would be the perfect excuse for casting someone younger!" giggled Titty.

"Naughty girl. Mind you, poor young Chris would have an easier time of it if that happened. Have you noticed how he cringes when he has to say those romantic words to his beautiful young Cinders while looking into Bunty's botox?"

"I'm not there for half of the rehearsals, Goody – not till costumes are needed. It was thoughtful of Greaty not to call us both in for every rehearsal. Having every other one off is such a blessing."

"So what do you get up to while Tony's out of the way?"

"Unfortunately, nothing," Titty sighs. "Because you-know-who isn't around when I'm free. For obvious reasons."

"Of course. Sorry."

"You're the lucky one. At least you get to spend more time with Greaty. Are you managing to make yourself indispensable?"

"I'm trying. I'm not sure he realises how much I do. He snaps his fingers and it's there, but he doesn't seem to see who brings it all to him. I'm dashing around like a mad thing some days. I wish I could drive but I'm sure I'd be hopeless."

"It's a pity you didn't keep up your cycling. You used to be a champion, didn't you?"

"Oh, that was ages ago. My old bike is rusting in the garage now. I should throw it away but I keep it for sentimental reasons."

"Talking of which, don't you have to take morning coffee to Jack and our Great Director?"

"Yikes! I must get going. Kiss, kiss. See you tomorrow."

I've already got her take-away order half prepared-it's always the same: three extra-hot white coffees, two almond croissants and a pain au raisin. She always has the foresight to bring her own flat-bottomed thermal bag so that the coffees don't spill during her twenty minute walk up there. Once she's packed her bag, she's off and almost running up to the new housing development where Greatorex and Jack will be working. Jack's small building firm does a lot of work for Greatorex & Tasley. (There's no Tasley any more, he's as dead as a doorbell, but Greaty thinks a partnership sounds more stable than a one-man-band.) G & T, as they're known locally, have developed most of the new properties here and Greaty has done well out of it. Jack's just a builder, though he's a proper one, don't get me wrong when I say 'just' a builder. It's only that he doesn't make as much money as Greaty. He's still quite expensive so lots of people go to Bertram for their odd jobs and small projects. Want a new house? Go to Greaty. Want a new bathroom? Go to Jack. Want some new tiles? Go to Bertram. See what I mean? Each one's got their place in the skills ladder. To each his bone.

Bertram works his odd jobs round his pub rota, so you have to wait till he can fit you in. Leela's using him at the moment in her flower shop, and Wendy's next in line for alterations to her wool shop. They're the next ones whose conversation you'll be interested in when they come in for coffee today.

"Jenny, darling, can I have a coffee and a large slice of that gorgeous chocolate fudge cake?" says Leela, eyeing the cakes greedily. "What about you, Wendy?"

"Maybe a wee almond tart. Black coffee," replies Wendy shyly, scurrying to claim a window table before anyone else comes in.

Wendy's a mouse of a thing. She's as thin as a rape and always seems to apologise if she eats anything. She twitches, too, from her nose to the tips of her fingers. If she's not knitting, she's twitching. Her life revolves around dressmaking and filling Christmas orders for complicated yuletide jumpers. Many a red-nosed reindeer has leapt from a swarthy chest due to Wendy's clickety-clicking. She loves panto time because she can pour all her fantasies into other people's costumes. Under her plain exterior, I think there might be a sparkling celebrity waiting to burst forth. You can't tell a book by its lover. She's a Kardashian in a cardigan. When I take the tray over to them, they're talking about Mimi at the last rehearsal.

"She did half the transformation scene with the underwire from her bra sticking up out of her cleavage! Did you see the men smirking?" asks a horrified Leela. "When I tried to point it out to her quietly, she just roared with laughter. Anyone who hadn't noticed before couldn't fail to see after that. So unnecessary."

"I think she enjoyed it," murmurs Wendy, pushing the sugar bowl well away from her.

I insert myself into the conversation. "Mind you, I hate those underwires myself. The first thing I do when I get home at night is to take off my bra," I say. "But it's so hard to get a pretty bra without those horrible metal underwires. And all the fancy ones are thimble sizes. I mean, who's a 32A nowadays?"

"I know," agrees Leela. "If you're over a 38, all you get is a choice of hammocks."

"I don't understand the department buyers. The average woman is a size 16 to 18 with a C or D cup bosom, but all the rails hold wispy dresses in size 8. Then along comes the Sale and all you can get are those teeny dresses that obviously haven't sold. Great for teenagers, but there must be a limit to the number of things they can buy even in a sale. You'd think the buyers would notice. Oh, sorry, I'm going off on one of my hobbyhorses when you just want to sit and chat quietly," I apologise.

"No, I agree. It drives me mad. You may not believe this, but I'm the same size as Marilyn Monroe," preens Leela. "She was a proper woman. You look at her in 'Some Like It Hot' – rounded boobs, full hips and an actual belly. Lovely. Half the models on the catwalks today could just as easily be adolescent boys. I often check to see if they've got Adam's apples."

Wendy is pretty quiet through this exchange. She could be one of the catwalkers with clothes hanging straight down from her shoulders, but she wouldn't have the confidence to do it. Bless.

"Just give me a call when you want the bill," I say airily as I return to the counter. They get straight down to business, talking about Bertram's work on their shops.

"All I wanted was new plaster on the basement walls. It's only used for storage. I just felt I couldn't put it on the market without smartening it up. But oh no, I have to have new plasterboard on new wooden battens – and he's acting like he's doing me a favour," complains Leela.

"That's what he said to me, too. Something about aluminium. His quote was much higher than I thought it would be. I might not bother to get it done. Trouble is, I store all my fabrics down there and I don't want them to get dusty. I don't know what to do."

"Dinna fash, hen. Come and look at mine when he's finished. If you don't think it's worth it, just cancel him."

"Good idea. Um, do you want half of my almond slice? I had an enormous breakfast and …"

"What? A whole slice of toast?" laughs Leela. "Give it here. Can't let good food go to waste. Not your waist, anyway, and I'm not too bothered about mine!"

"I don't want to alter your costumes, though!" smiles Wendy.

"I thought you'd be measuring me for a shroud the other day – I got stung by a bee who must have been kipping in the petals and you know how allergic I am. I had my epipen right there, so all was well."

"It must be so difficult for you. Aren't there bees buzzing around your flowers all the time?"

"The wonderful thing about bees is that they won't sting you unless you bother them. They leave their sting behind, you know, and then they're done for. So as long as you're careful and don't panic, you're fine," Leela assures her. "I'm always telling Bertram but he still goes into fits if he sees a bee."

"Is he allergic, too?"

"Apparently. That's why he says he doesn't like outside jobs in the summer. My goodness, this almond slice is delicious. Jenny!" she calls out to me. "Is this home-made, too?"

"Everything is home-made. Tom and I spend hours every evening baking for your delectation," I say. She really should know that by now, but it doesn't hurt to re-iterate it.

"You're lucky with your Tom. My husband deigns to wash up but that's it. I only got him to do that because having my hands in water at the shop all day was wreaking havoc with my rheumatism. Still, some men won't even do that, will they?"

Wendy nods vigourously at that, as if she knew all about men and their vicissitudes. Bless. Her whole life is pins and needles, without a prick in sight. She knits a sweater for Jack every birthday but that's as close as she gets. I suppose she has the pleasure of measuring up the men every panto, if you can call that a pleasure. Most of them need a hose down. Poor old Wendy. Tom tells me off whenever I say that, because he thinks some people are happier on their own than in a marriage. He's probably right, looking round at some of the relationships in Middle Pidding.

"When are you going to tell people you're selling the flower shop, Leela? Can you think of anyone to take it over?" asks Wendy.

"Not a word about it yet, pet. I don't want people knowing till I've done it up a bit. Old Mrs Grainger has a grand-daughter who works in the flower shop in Walmsley Ayrton. I'm hoping Granny might set her up in her own business. I'm a great believer in handing the dosh down before you die. Makes more sense than leaving it to the District Nurse!"

"Ooh, Leela, you are naughty!" giggles Wendy, like a schoolgirl hearing a bit of ribald gossip about one of her teachers. "Don't let Mimi hear you say that!"

"She's benefitted from a good few bequests. The Morton family are still sore about the jewellery their grandma left to her."

"You don't think there was any coercion involved, do you?" asks Wendy with bated breath, longing for a thrilling piece of gossip.

"I couldn't say. All I know is that the flowers from Mimi that I did for the funeral were accidentally trampled on by Gerry Morton!"

The shop suddenly becomes over-run with a coach party visiting the area. I know I should be grateful because it's always lucrative, but their chatter blocks out everything else. I don't even see Wendy and Bunty leave.

The last conversation in the shop that day is one you'll find interesting before we get to the **murder.** It is one I have with our local reporter, Jane Makepeace. She pops in to check a couple of facts for an article she's writing. She's just a kid really but she's very enthusiastic. The Greta Thunberg of Walmsley Ayrton. The local editor sends her out to cover anything rural so she's usually here for the Produce Show and the Best Garden Competition. She's desperate to find skulduggery behind the hedgerows – you know, farmers using sprays that are toxic to wildlife and that sort of thing. She thought she was onto something big a while back when some very nasty poisonous stuff found its way into the local streams. Someone had dumped chemicals and no-one was owning up to it, unsurprisingly. Jane took up her crusading banners and marched on Greaty. Why? Well, he'd just finished building a small estate on what had been the local chemical plant. In came the Inspectors, making Greaty's life a misery and examining everything but his toenail cuttings. They found nothing, of course, and had no success in tracing who'd dumped the toxic waste. No slur on Greatorex & Tasley, and Greaty was able to put his new-built houses on the market. It was touch and go for a while because people's fears had been aroused, but after he'd lowered the prices a bit all the houses sold. I don't think he and Jane are the best of friends, though. He called her Jane Make-a-piece-up for weeks afterwards. Fortunately, she doesn't live in our Village so the stink (literally) died down. Bless her cock and socks, her heart's in the right place and she really cares about the 'henvironment', but she sometimes doesn't engage her brain before she opens her mouth.

"I don't see you in Pidding very often, young Jane. What's occurring?, as they say?" I ask her.

"I've been asked to write a piece on the Pantomime," she says, flopping into a chair with a despairing air. "I can't think of anything worse!"

"Thank you very much!"

"Oh, there I go again. Foot straight into mouth. I don't mean I think the panto will be bad, but I really don't want to ask Greatorex Manston for anything, not after our last skirmish."

"Have a jam doughnut, love, and I'll give you all the background you need."

She really shouldn't have a doughnut, given that her forehead looks like the foothills of the Himalayas. All those hormones rushing around trying to burst out. Who'd be a teenager again, eh? But she needs a bit of comforting before tackling that job, and there's nothing better than jam oozing out of a doughnut to achieve that. A little of what you fancy does you pud.

"Oh thanks, Mrs Brandon, you're a star."

"No, I'm the Prompt," I say, and that brings a tiny smile to her chubby face. When she smiles, she's as pretty as a pitcher.

"All I've got to do this time is tell the avid public who's playing what and if there's anything exciting happening. If you can help me with that, I won't have to go near Mr Manston. The worst bit is going to be when I do a puff nearer the time, interviewing some of the principals. I mean, I can hardly avoid talking to the bloody Director then, can I? Nightmare!"

She wrapped her sturdy legs round the chair's sturdy legs and took a very large bite of doughnut. The sugar moustache made her look about ten years old. Bless.

"I can give you a printed cast list, petal, so you'll have no worries about getting the names wrong. I'll give you the dates of the shows and the Box Office phone number. Anything else?"

"Is there anything new, anything different, anything exciting?" she asks hopefully. "Or is it the same old crowd?"

"Careful, dear. Never use the word 'old' when you refer to our illustrious thespians."

"Sorry. But it would be nice to have a new name on the list."

"You're in luck. We have a handsome Prince who really is handsome. Young Chris Monk. Do you know him?"

"Wow!" she says, sugary jaw dropping. The sight of masticating doughnut is not pretty. "He's gorgeous. Black is beautiful and all that. I had no idea he was a member of the Dramatic Society. That's brilliant. I can do an interview with him asking him how he got involved and what he thinks about the play."

"Let's hope he isn't too truthful. Or if he is, let's hope you've learnt your lesson and you don't actually print it. Get my meaning?"

"Sure, Mrs Brandon. Depend on me to be the soul of tact. As long as I get a good photo of him, no-one will take any notice of what I've written anyway! I'll label it "The Black Prince!"

And off she goes, cast list in hand, rushing back a moment later to get Chris's address and phone number. Good luck to her, say I.

Chapter 6

The very next day, Chris Monk strides into the shop. His handsome jaw is a little clenched and I'm thinking he's not here for a lunchtime snack.

"I have a little bone to pick with you, Jenny," he says.

"What would that be, Chris dear?"

"I believe you divulged my address and phone number to a reporter."

"Ah, yes I did. I didn't think you'd mind being interviewed about your part in the panto – in fact, I thought you'd be pleased."

"I wasn't pleased that she just turned up without warning on my doorstep. I had a friend there and he opened the door, only to have a camera thrust into his face. I was pretty angry, I can tell you. It was just plain rude," he fumes.

"I'm so sorry," I apologise, "I thought she'd have the sense to phone you to make an appointment. I should have realised her youthful enthusiasm would override her manners. My mistake. Have a sausage roll and a coffee on the house. Were you able to sort it out?"

"My friend was none too happy but I got rid of the reporter quite quickly in the end. I gave her the usual guff about being thrilled about my first part, she took another photo, and off she went. But it shouldn't have happened, Jenny."

At that moment, Bertram comes in for a lunchtime take-away and he clocks the strained atmosphere. He puts his arm round Chris's shoulders and tells him he's just the man he wanted to see and what a happy co-incidence it is. He leads him to a table and winks at me. I don't particularly like the man, but he did me a good turn there. I take Chris's freebies over and then I hurry back to the counter to make Bertram's ham and coleslaw sandwich (he has either that or a large sausage roll every day, which may sound boring if you haven't tasted one of my home-cured ham and special coleslaw-with-peeled-apple-chunks-and-plump-raisins delights!) My Tom comes down for his lunch at the same time which means I don't hear what Bertram wants to talk to Chris about, so I can't fill you in on that piece of information. When I glance back, Bertram is just putting a notebook back in his pocket, except that he misses the pocket and it slips onto the floor. Many a slip between cup and hip. I was just about to tell him when I got an inkling that it might be interesting to look at it. Yes, I know that was naughty but looking back I'm very glad I did. You'll be pleased, too, because it has something to do with the **murder**. I wrap up Bertram's sandwich and he gives me the right money, as usual, and he and Chris go off together. As I'm cleaning the table, I surreptitiously pick up the notebook and put it in my capacious apron pocket to look at later that night.

Tom and I huddle over it after our evening meal – curry, tastily made by Tom. Mostly, the book is full of shopping lists and paint colours for jobs he's done. There are prices for plasterboard and batten wood, which must be for Leela and Wendy's basements, along with their respective phone numbers. There are prices for burglar alarms and peepholes and a list of people, some of whom I happen to know have had Bertram fit intruder alarms for them after there were some petty thefts in the village. He did pretty well out of that little scare as the police were useless at finding out who the thief was. Tom had quite a lot of insurance claims to process after the incidents, so he was well aware of who got done. He laughingly suggested that Bertram might have been the thief so he could increase his intruder alarm business! We thought it was a joke at the time but now I'm not so sure. The **murder** opened our eyes to all sorts of possibilities. You get to know all about people's inner lives if you scratch beneath the surface. You never really know what goes on behind closed floors.

However, there's one page of the notebook which we can't make head nor tail of. This is it

"What the hell is that?" puzzles Tom.

	ML	GD	JX	EC	LX	WX	RC
1			//	//	//		
8	//		//			//	
15							
22	//	//	//	//	//	//	//
	100	500	30	200	20	20	100
POSSIBLE CX?							

We both screw our eyes up, hold the page right up close and then at arm's length, turn it on its side and

even upside down. Neither of us has got any idea.
Maybe we can't see the wood for the treats.

"Let's think about it as we make tomorrow's
goodies," I say eventually. "Maybe something will
pop into our heads while we work. That often
happens with crossword clues."

I set about the coleslaw, peeling the apples,
chopping the cabbage, soaking the sultanas to
plump them up. Once I've shredded, I do an extra
chop so that each shred is quite short: no-one wants
to bite into a sandwich and have lengths of cabbage
spilling down their chin. I'm sure that's why my
coleslaw is so popular: people just don't want to be
embarrassed by dangling shreds. Our mayonnaise is
made every few days – with the best ingredients –
so stirring it all together is a real pleasure. While
I'm doing that, Tom is folding finely chopped apple
into the sausage meat ready for the sausage rolls.
We make jumbo rolls for the shop so that one makes
a substantial lunch. When we do a catering event,
of course, we make dainty ones – but Wendy is the
only person who would consider a petite one as an
adequate meal! All the while we're mixing, we're
chatting about the notebook.

"I notice that the numbers on the left are seven apart. That could be dates in a month, couldn't it?" I theorise.

"Could be. So that would denote the 1st, 8th, 15th and 22nd. Maybe they're meetings," replies Tom.

"The letters are strange. I thought at first they might be people's initials until I realised that four of them would have a surname starting with an X."

"Only three, surely?"

"Four if you count CX at the bottom."

"That just can't be right. There aren't four people in the neighbourhood with an X for a surname. In fact, I can't even think of a name beginning with an X," says Tom.

"There's Xavier. But that's a first name."

"I've finished the sausage mixture. I'll have a quick look in the telephone directory," says Tom, washing his hands.

Of course, there's nothing. So we're stuck. We look again at the numbers at the bottom. Tom thinks it might be points awarded for something, in which case GD is the winner. I say it could be money, but surely you'd expect a pound sign if it was. We're completely flummoxed.

"Could they be payments? So ML made two payments…" I start

"…that totalled £100," finishes Tom.

"But EC also made two payments, and that came to £200. So that's a bit puzzling."

"And inconsistent."

"Are we thinking that Bertram might be a blackmailer?" I suggest.

"That's a very un-P.C. word, dear. You have to say extortionist nowadays," reprimands Tom, not entirely seriously.

"I suppose it could just as easily be money he paid out rather money he collected in," I muse.

"Unlikely. If they were payments out it would mean that this particular month he spent £970. He probably doesn't earn much more than that, even with extras from odd jobs, does he?"

"Surely not. He wouldn't have had time to do that number of odd jobs, anyway. He's still working on Leela's basement – and her initials aren't down there. I mean, there's an L but it's followed by an

X. It would be LD, not LX, if it was Leela. And her work will be costing much more than twenty quid, too. So these must have been receipts from things other than work."

"If they're receipts at all. As you said, there's no pound sign," adds Tom.

"I'd better give the notebook back to him at the next rehearsal, I suppose."

Tom catches the note of reluctance in my voice and says, "Hang on to it for a bit. He won't know he dropped it in the café. We can always give it back later and say we found it in the street or something. I'd like to give it further thought. I don't like to be beaten by a puzzle."

So that's what we did. I know it was naughty but we honestly didn't think it was important. It was just a notebook. In fact, it turned out to be a major piece of evidence after the **murder** so it was just as well we did hang on to it. The law of unexpected consequences.

"I was surprised to see how angry Chris was about your giving his address to little Miss Makepeace," says Tom. "I mean, we all know where he lives. It isn't a great secret. She could have found out from anyone."

"Yeah, his anger seemed out of proportion. Perhaps it was the fact that she didn't phone him first to see if it was convenient."

"I suppose so. But if it were me, I'd be angry at her rather than you. Don't you think his reaction was a bit over-the-top? Could he have been cross that his friend who opened the door was embarrassed? Any idea who it was?"

"No. Probably someone from his work. Anyway, from the way little Miss Makepeace dashed off from here, I think she may have a bit of a crush on our handsome Prince Charming. She's only about nineteen. Probably led a sheltered life, too. The thought of getting up close and personal to him must have been so tempting. Poor kid," says I, remembering my own teenage crushes.

"You'd think he'd be a bit more understanding about her youth. I can imagine her looking up at him from the doorstep with starry eyes. He should have been flattered. I'd have lapped it up," laughs Tom.

"It wasn't him who opened the door, though. It was this friend who obviously didn't like his photo being taken without warning."

"I'm still wondering who that was. Or what he was trying to hide," says Tom thoughtfully.

"Never mind, let's get on with the cooking. You do the jumbo sausage rolls – the pastry's in the fridge – and I'll make gingerbread."

"Don't let your gannets have all of it. Save at least one piece for me tomorrow!"

"Of course. I'm only making it because it's your favourite."

Chapter 7

I'm moving you on now to the end of our seventh dress rehearsal. Yes, seventh. I know most productions survive with just a couple but Greaty says, quite rightly in my opinion, that a good panto has got to flow smoothly and look seamless. There's a lot of slapstick where the timing has got to be immaculate. You can rehearse it time and again and think you've got it perfectly, but as soon as you're in costume it all feels different. Men aren't used to wearing long dresses, for instance, so the Ugly Sisters need to get used to the way it hampers your walk. The first time Robbie had to dance in the Ball regalia, he fell smack on his face and ripped his petticoat. Poor Wendy. Bless. That needle of hers was working overtime that evening. She just quietly got on with the repairs while Robbie ranted on about never wanting to play a Dame again. A stitch in time saves knives. Robbie was nervous because he reckoned his pub receipts would go down when customers saw him in lipstick and a wig, but we all assured him that people would find it a hoot and go to the pub even more often to tease him. Not that that made him any happier. So you can see that multiple dress rehearsals are essential.

By the end of the seventh, the cast are all exhausted, and part of Greaty's job is to give them his notes on the performance without upsetting them too much, pouring oil over troubled warders, and giving everyone a Prince Fillip.

"Well done, darlings. Get out of your cossies quickly –but carefully –and come and sit down."

"He said charily," said Robbie.

There's a general bustle and lots of swearing as they hang their costumes up on Wendy's rack (if you'll pardon the expression). As always, there are rips to be mended and Fabreze to be liberally applied. It always amazes me how much men sweat but still insist they don't need an anti-perspirant. Do they think it's effeminate to smell nice? Chris is the only one who departs as immaculately as he came, but then he's 'next generation'.

Freddy appears to have lost yet another button from his final costume, and as he's playing Buttons it's rather important. Wendy had found him a set of large gold ones for his walk-down costume which are irreplaceable as they're genuine 1940s, so there they are on hands and knees searching the floor for the one that's gone AWOL. Everyone else is trying to avoid treading on them and nearly always succeeding. The odd yelp indicates the failures.

"I'm ever so sorry, Wend. I think I caught it on the door handle when I came on," he whines.

"Then shouldn't we be looking over there? Why did you pick this spot to search?" says a puzzled Wendy.

"Well, there's more light over here," he replies absurdly.

"Wendy, love," shouts Robbie, "I think my wig has lost a lot of its bounce. It needs to be more bouffant. Can you have a go at it? Yours could do with a fluff up, too, Bertram."

"He said airily," quips Bertram. "Here, can someone undo my zip? I think there's a bit of lace stuck in it."

"He said fixedly," Robbie quips back.

Mimi is staring in the mirror, appraising her ample torso from one side then another before saying, "I think there are more sequins on my left than my right."

"That's because your left boob is bigger," says Bunty. "Everybody's got one larger than the other.

I'd have thought you would have known that, with all your medical training."

"Mine must be exceptional, then," she preens.

"Cor, you can say that again," leers Jack, and his remark is picked up by poor Wendy, who looks as though he's just slapped her. I don't think she'll ever accept that Jack isn't interested in her, no matter how many sweaters she knits for him. Mimi's boobs will win every time and she knows it. All's fair in love and warts.

"Can you just put a few more sequins on?" continues Mimi. "I don't think the Fairy Godmother can ever be thought of as over-the-top, can she?"

"Just over the hill," mutters Bunty.

Chris, ever the gentleman, is helping Titty to extricate herself from the horse's front end. Tony looks daggers at him but he can't do anything about it because he's pretty tied up in the back end. I notice she's rubbing her behind and I wonder if Tony's been pinching her bum while under cover of the costume. I wouldn't put it past him, he can be a vicious bugger at times. She used to give as good as she got, but I've noticed recently that she just lets it go. Tom reckons she's filling her nosebag elsewhere, but the only person she talks to is Goody and she's keeping schtum.

Greaty is being terribly patient waiting for his ragtag cast to hang up their togs. It's Goody who flaps around trying to hurry everyone up. She seems to feel responsible for every moment of his wasted time. Bless. He doesn't seem to register. She's the classic P.A. who's taken for granted by her unthinking boss. Tom reckons that she should let someone else stage manage the next play just to show him how efficient she is in contrast. Maybe then he'd realise what a treasure he's got. She won't, of course. I don't think she could bear it if someone else was having all those meetings with him, giving him advice and opinions, running around making his life easy. And, heaven forfend, but suppose this new person was just as good or even better? Goody would be devastated.

"Are we nearly ready, people?" he says hopefully, shuffling his papers.

The short answer is No. It's still a bit of a bear garden. You may be wondering why everyone is changing in the hall rather than in the dressing rooms. For a start, there is only one dressing room and at the moment it's full of extra lights that Jack is still deciding if he needs or not, boxes of frills and furbelows which might come in handy for Wendy, alternative props if Greaty doesn't like what Goody has sourced, and a broken harness for Horse. It's like the wreck of the Hesperus in there. So as the waiting time gets longer, the tempers get shorter. At the back of our minds is the knowledge that all that stuff in the dressing room will have to be cleared out and stored away tonight after Greaty's notes. It will be needed as a proper dressing room tomorrow for the first of two Final Dress Rehearsals (the irony of that sentence is not lost on me!)

"While you're still changing," calls Greaty, "don't forget that we'll want full make-up tomorrow."

"Even for the Uglies?" asks Robbie.

"Especially for the Uglies," says Greaty firmly. "Eyes, cheeks, lips."

"And can I remind you to put chiffon scarves over your heads when you're changing so your make-up doesn't stain your costumes. I shall have enough to do without trying to remove lipstick from all the lace and satin," urges Wendy with as much force as she's capable of – which isn't a lot.

"If we're doing full slap, we must have the dressing room cleared. We'll need to be sitting in front of the mirrors," shouts Bunty, looking hard at Goody, who's looking more flustered than usual.

Greaty continues: "And Jane What's-her-name …"

"Makepeace," supplies Goody.

"She'll be coming in to interview a few of you for the local paper's splash about the panto. It won't take long, but it must be endured if we want the paper to give us a big spread. Goody and I will meet her first to stuff her full of tea and biscuits. It's a pity she's just the Gardening Correspondent but she can't do much harm."

"Unless she starts going on about the "henvironment", as she calls it," laughs Mimi in a veiled dig at the chemical spill fiasco. Fortunately, Greaty doesn't seem to catch on.

At last everyone is changed and seated, ready for Greaty's notes. We're all praying he won't go on too long.

"On the whole, I thought it went very well." (Everyone preens.) "But there are one or two little comments." (Everyone groans.) "First of all, this was our first performance with all the lights. I'm sure we all want to say thank you to Jack for such a sterling effort." (Half-hearted murmurs of approval.)

"I've made some notes for meself," says Jack, hoping that Greaty will leave it at that and not criticise him in front of the cast. No such luck.

"I did ask for a pink filter for Cinderella. Just to emphasise her lovely complexion. Where was that tonight? And up stage right was far too gloomy – I could hardly see the Fairy Godmother when she first came on."

"He said darkly," says Bertram.

Mimi looks annoyed and is obviously just about to remonstrate with Jack when he quickly assures her that he's already dealt with that while everyone was changing.

"And, people, you need to find your lights. It's no good Jack putting up a lovely spotlight if you don't stand in it. That's mostly you, Chris. Remember, if you stand at the back edge of the spot, your face won't be lit. Stand near the front of it – we need to see your handsome visage."

"Yes," agrees Jack. "Your colour just disappears into the dark." (Was that racist? Hard to tell with Jack.)

"Lastly, Jack, I know we agreed to lower the lights for scene changes, but the poor darlings need to be able to see where they're going. Goody nearly went arse over tip bringing on the pumpkin. Oh, and can that pumpkin be more orange than pink? Realism, darling, realism! I've never seen a pink pumpkin, have you?"

Goody hurriedly makes a note, for it will be she who has to mix a colour suitable for Greaty's idea of orange.

"Now, on to the cast. All of you need to jump onto your cues more quickly. I could have driven a coach and horses through some of those pauses. Snap, snap, snap. Cues, cues, cues."

"Sounds like a vegetable stall," mutters Bertram.

"He said leekily," adds Robbie.

"Now I'm very pleased with the way you've perfected your moves, but be careful not to anticipate. Bunty, you were walking towards the door before anyone had knocked; and Leela, the telephone has to ring before you pick it up. There was one telephone mishap that was straight out of Acorn Antiques."

Bunty and Leela bridle and are quick to get in with their excuses. It's always someone else's fault.

"The knocker was late," says Bunty. "I couldn't just stand there waiting."

"So was the telephone," says Leela. "I picked it up because I thought it had been forgotten."

"Goody, make a note of that, please."

Poor Goody, she knows that neither excuse is true but she just has to suck it up. Frankly, that's why I'd never want to be an S.M. – everyone blames you when things go wrong, and things always go wrong so you're always being blamed.

"Tony," continues Greaty, "you forgot to wag Horse's tail whenever Cinderella talked to you. Is there a problem with the mechanism?"

"Ooh, Tony, have you got trouble with your mechanism?" asks Freddy with a cheeky grin on his face.

"It's just hard to hear anything in there. Everything's muffled," sulks Tony, ignoring Freddy completely.

"Perhaps you could cue him in, Titty. Wiggle your b.t.m at the appropriate moment," suggests Greaty.

"Anything you say, boss," she replies between extremely gritted teeth.

"While we're on the Horse – so to speak – I was expecting the harness tonight. The whole point of not having a golden coach is that the harness stretches into the wings as if there was a coach on the end of it. Without that, it looks as though Cinders is going to go off on horseback."

Goody explains nervously that she was standing there in the wings ready to hold on to the ropes but Jack had told her not to use the harness tonight.

"Why the hell not? Where is the confounded thing?" asks Greaty.

"It's in the dressing room," she squeaks.

"I 'aven't had time to mend it, mate. I'll do it tomorrow morning. It'll be all right for the evening."

We're all starting to feel a wee bit uncomfortable. We've noticed that Greaty is introducing a few choice words into his questions. Goody offers him a mollifying Jelly Baby. It's like watching kids in the playground. Let's hope that biting the head off a sweet will stop him from doing the same to one of us.

"Mimi, I gave you this note yesterday, but it seems I'll have to say it again. You need to make much more of your song "Nobody Loves a Fairy When She's Forty". You're still singing it as if you <u>are</u> forty. The whole joke is that you're way over forty and the audience has to know that you know that they know and are making a laugh out of it. Do you see?"

We're all holding our breath, wondering if Mimi will react. It could mean tears, or it could mean tantrums. Mimi is very sensitive about her age and she's very vulnerable tonight because one of her patients died yesterday and she always takes it to heart. Fortunately, she just glares at Greaty and he sweeps on.

"Chris, you're not lovestruck enough. Every time you're near Cinders we need to feel the heat of your desire."

Someone snorts. We've all seen how Chris backs away from the lovely Leela, looking as if he'd rather be wooing a bow constructer. You can't blame him, she must be at least thirty years older than him. Leela's eyes narrow – we've seen that look before, and it usually comes before an eruption.

"Sorry," says Chris quickly. "I was worried about my breath. Too much garlic at lunchtime."

Good lad. That might just be enough to appease the goddess. She smiles and we all relax.

"Don't worry about that, darling. I promise not to flinch," she purrs.

"It's called acting, Chris. All right?" snaps Greaty.

"Finally," (sighs of relief) "we spent a long time identifying when the laughs will come. You all know to wait for the next line until the laughter is just dying down. What we haven't done yet is to think about possible heckling. I must say this is an aspect of panto that I thoroughly dislike. Nobody would dream of calling out during 'The Three Sisters' but they feel it's allowed in panto."

"Sod off to Moscow!" shouts Bertram. We start to laugh until we see that Greaty is doing a Queen Victoria, definitely not amused.

"We give them leave to call out 'Look behind you' and those ridiculous 'Yes she is', 'No she isn't' sequences but some of them take it too far. If anyone shouts out a ribald comment, you must just ignore it and carry on. No ad libbing."

Actually, most of us quite like the odd ad lib. It gives a bit of spice to the mix and we're pretty good at witty rejoinders. But Greaty thinks it turns a script into a stand-up and he won't have any of it. Tight-arse!

"Well, I think that's it. I just want perfection tomorrow, people. That's all I'm asking." (He has the decency to smile.) "Now go home, get a good night's sleep and bounce in tomorrow ready to wow me. Oh, and don't forget there'll be about fifteen minutes with Jane Whatsit beforehand. Don't be late!"

Five minutes later, it's just us back-stagers left. The cast have gone off to the pub and soon they'll all be pissed as a mute. We're the Mugginses who have to clear out the dressing room and get the props in place for the first Final Dress, or the Semi-final Final Dress as Jack calls it. Even Greaty says he's too tired to stay on as he has to 'prepare himself' for tomorrow night. As soon as he's gone, Jack mutters something about how exhausting it must be to sit there all night watching other people work. So there's me, Jack, Goody and Wendy facing the chaos that is the Dressing Room. Actually, Wendy has her work cut out to nurse the costumes back to health, so it's really just the three of us in the wreckage. I pop into the loo (we have a spanking new unisex one) and give Tom a surreptitious call to see if he feels like adding his rested muscles to our weary ones. I do it secretly just in case he doesn't feel like coming out in the winter cold. I wouldn't want the others knowing if he says Niet. Fortunately for all of us, Barkis is willing and he's here in ten minutes. Bless.

"Blimey, mate, am I glad to see you," says Jack as soon as he claps eyes on Tom. "These flaming lights are 'eavy and they live up in the loft. If you can pass them up to me, we can get it done really fast."

Wendy twitters a greeting from behind a mist of Fabreze while Goody and I start shifting props into the tiny Props Room. I really don't know why she resurrected some of these things. I mean, why on earth would Cinderella need a rifle that has a flag saying BANG dropping down when you pull the trigger? Or a canoe paddle? She gets a bit carried away at times.

"I expect there's rhyme and reason behind your storage, Goody. Do you want to tell me where to put things, or shall I just bring things to you to put away in the right places?"

"Let's bring an armful each and sort them out together," she says. "Then we can have a chat as we work."

So that's what we do, balancing fans and vases and broomsticks as we circumvent lights and chairs. Back in the Props Room, Goody obviously has something on her mind.

"Jenny, you know Jane Makepeace is coming in tomorrow to do the newspaper article? Well, I was wondering if you would help me steer her away from mentioning the chemical dumping from last year."

"That's all over and done with now, isn't it? She got her fingers burnt pushing too hard at it – I happen to know the Editor was very cross with her for stirring up so much trouble. I think she was lucky to keep her job."

"That's true, but she's so young and impetuous. Sometimes these youngsters just don't know when to keep their mouths shut. I can see her saying something stupid and accusing Greaty and Jack all over again."

"They were exonerated, love. We all know that."

"Yes, but Greaty mustn't be distracted with the panto so close to opening. And Jack was so upset by it all, I was really worried about him. The environment police interrogated him for hours until he was a nervous wreck," she frets.

"Ah, there's Big Sister sticking up for her little brother – again. I hope Jack knows how lucky he is to have you always there for him."

"He's had a few scrapes in the past, but he's making a real success of his business now. I'm so proud of him, Jenny. Greaty's been able to give him a lot of work."

"Thanks to you, no doubt," I say.

"It's always fair and square, with proper tendering. It's just that it makes all our lives easier if I'm a go-between. Pass me the beehive, will you?"

"What panto did that come into?"

"Oh, it didn't. Greaty wanted to see if it would fit into 'The Cherry Orchard',"

"The what?" I ask.

"You know, Chekhov. Greaty is thinking about doing it next summer."

"It's a bit highbrow for us, isn't it?"

"Greaty says that people don't understand how funny Chekhov is. Shall we go and get another armful?"

Three more trips see the Dressing Room cleared and me fully informed about the plot of 'The Cherry Orchard'. By that time, Jack and Tom are onto the last lantern and Wendy is finishing the mammoth task of hanging the costumes in the Dressing Room, carefully separating each character's cossies and placing them together on the rails. Jack takes the broken harness into the hall while the rest of us do a quick clean-up, wiping the surfaces, hoovering and polishing the mirrors. Our thespians will have nothing to complain about, though that won't stop them. They're a moany lot till the Opening Night, when suddenly they're best mates and can't do enough to help each other out. I always think it's a pity that there aren't more performances because I love the supportive family we all become during the show. Everyone is totally reliant on everyone else and it brings out the best. Mind you, it isn't the best that comes out at the next rehearsal, but the **murderous** worst.

Chapter 8

Are you ready for the day of the **murder**? It was a
fairly ordinary day with nothing special occurring.
Everyone involved in the panto was experiencing
that weird mixture of nerves and excitement that is
part and parcel of a production Dress Rehearsal,
with the added mixed feelings of having Jane
Makepeace there taking down people's quotable
quotes. I dash home at closing time to dress in
black – no, I'm not in mourning; it's a theatrical
convention that workers backstage wear black so
they don't get seen by the audience. When I arrive
at the hall, Jack has arranged some chairs round in a
semi-circle so we can to talk to Jane, and most
people are there. Greaty's told them to be in mufty
for the interviews and photographs, though I notice
that Leela and Mimi are looking very well-dressed
and have put on quite a lot of their eye make-up
already. Mutton dressed as spam. Could that have
anything to do with the presence of a camera, do
you think? You know them by now, so enough
said!

Greaty sweeps in with Goody and Jane in his slipstream.

"Greetings, lovely people," he says, oozing charm. "Are we all present and correct?"

"I did email everyone to remind them it was a seven o'clock start," apologises Goody, desperate not to be the one who is to blame for any non-attendance.

"We'll just start with the faithful, shall we?" beams Greaty, ushering Jane to a seat. "Now, where's our Cinders?"

Leela waves coquettishly, doing that funny little wave that just involves fingers. I suppose from a very great distance you might think she was youngish. Jane stares for just a moment too long, so we all know she's noticed the inappropriateness of the casting.

"I've been playing panto Princesses for a while, so I know my way around," she assures Jane.

"You can say that again," mutters Robbie.

"So you're doing a more mature interpretation of the story, are you?" asks Jane innocently. (Or is it?)

"Pardon?"

Greaty steps in quickly: "No, no, it's a straightforward version and Leela is our lovely Cinders. Next to her is Robbie Slack, one of the Ugly Sisters."

"I model myself on my wife, Alice. Oops, what I mean is that I've watched her carefully to get the femininity of the character. Please don't put that in your article – she may misunderstand."

Jane smiles. "Who is your sibling?"

Robbie looks confused. You don't need a wide vocabulary behind the bar and Robbie certainly hasn't got one.

"Bertram hasn't arrived yet," apologises Goody, looking a bit rattled. She's also noticed that Chris, Freddy and Titty aren't here either. Poor lamb, Greaty will eat her for breakfast.

"We do have the Wicked Stepmother, who is marvellously villainous," offers the embattled Goody.

"Oh, you're playing the stepmum as a drag role, too, are you?" asks wide-eyed Jane. (Now I'm sure she's not innocent!)

Bunty jerks her head up. "What?"

"Bunty is a stepmother in real life," gushes Goody. "That's what she models her performance on."

"Pardon me?" says Bunty stonily.

"I mean it's just the opposite of her real life. You have to know good before you can portray wicked, don't you?" flounders Goody.

I've never seen her so flustered. I have to step in to save her.

"You'll know everyone from the cast list that I gave you, Jane. There's Mimi. The Fiery Fairy Godmother, and Tony the Horse's arse..."

"No Prince Charming yet?" she asks. "No Buttons?"

"She said zippily," says Robbie.

"And where's Titty?" asks Greaty, looking crossly at Tony.

"She'll be here soon. I'm afraid Titania suffers badly from migraines and had to go home early from the Off Licence that we run. Oh, by the way, if you ever have a party we can do sale or return and throw in the glasses."

"Don't throw them in, Tony dear," smiles Mimi, "or poor Jack will have to sweep it all up."

"Who's Jack?" queries Jane, looking round.

"That's me. I do the lights and build the sets."

"Ah, a builder in real life as well as for the panto. I must remember that - my mum's patio needs some TLC," Jane smiles, as if she doesn't remember him from the chemical fiasco.

"I could work on that for you," he says.

"He said constructively," quips Robbie.

Remembering Goody's plea that we keep Jane off the subject of building in case the chemical spill rears its ugly hedge, I'm about to move her on to Wendy's costumes, when Chris comes rushing in closely followed by Freddy.

"I'm so sorry," he pants. "My train abandoned us way before this station because there was an 'incident', which usually means someone jumped onto the track. I was absolutely stuck. I phoned Freddy so he could tell you what had happened and he heroically offered to drive miles over to me and pick me up."

Freddy looks at Chris adoringly (Hello, I thought) and says, "It was the least I could do. He'd never have made it otherwise."

"Buttons and the Prince!" announces Greaty triumphantly. "We're just missing an Ugly Sister and the front end of the Horse. I suggest you start your mini interviews, Jane. We can only allow you half an hour, I'm afraid. There's a little polishing to be done to our gem of a panto after you've gone."

"Fair enough," says Jane, who's obviously very happy that Chris has turned up. "But do you mind if I go to the loo first? Too many cups of tea."

"Of course. Goody will show you to our new unisex toilet."

Off they go, and as soon as they're out of the hall, Greaty drops his smile and glares at Tony. "Would it be too much trouble for you to phone your wife and ask her to bloody well get her arse in gear?"

"I've been doing that. But I'll try again."

Suddenly, there's a piercing scream from the corridor and Goody and Jane rush back in.

"He's dead. He's dead!" sobs Goody.

"Who?" we all chorus.

"It's Bertram. No wonder he wasn't here to be interviewed."

"Not only dead," says Jane. "But it looks like **murder** to me!"

Chapter 9

As you can imagine, we're all stunned for a moment or two. You could knock me down with a leather. Greaty is the first to raise his dropping jaw.

"Murder? What do you mean?"

"Well, there isn't a dagger sticking out of his back …" gasps Jane.

"She said pointedly," jokes Robbie, and then looks ashamed for making light of a serious situation.

"… but that swollen mouth with the tongue sticking out…"

We're all shuddering by now, holding on to one another with sheer disbelief on our faces. We're thinking it can't be true, not in Middle Pidding.

Jack turns to Mimi, who is always a stalwart in times of medical emergency. "Perhaps you'd better take a look, Mimi. With all that nursing training, you'll know a natural dead 'un from a done-in one."

"Just so there are two of you – you know, to witness each other –perhaps Bunty should go, too," says Greaty sensibly.

Off they trot, leaving the rest of us poised between shock and disbelief. Murmurs start bubbling up about phoning the police but Leela suggests that we should wait till the girls come back just in case it's a natural death and all we have to do is phone Doc Patel.

"Poor old Bertram. He'd seemed so much happier lately, as if he'd turned his life around," muses Leela.

All our eyes are on the corridor door leading to the kitchen and the loo, just waiting for Mimi and Bunty to come back with their verdict.

"Phone the police immediately," orders Bunty. "It looks like poison to me."

It's what we've been dreading to hear and no-one moves at first. Then everybody is reaching for their phones at the same time until Greaty takes charge and says he'll do it. Little Jane starts crying, no doubt re-living the sight of her first murdered body. She runs to Mimi for comfort. Between sobs, she's holding out her bloodstained hand and I'm hoping she didn't actually touch the body. It turns out that she scratched her hand on the loo doorhandle. All it needs is a tiny plaster, but she's too upset to be able to put it into context and to her it seems like the end of the world. Bless. Mimi tries to cheer her up by chatting to her about anything and nothing.

"Last time I had to use my training was when one of our directors fell off the stage. Do you remember, Bunty? It was the Dress Rehearsal of some Noel Coward thing."

"It was 'Present Laughter'," supplies Bunty. "We had to patch up his ankle, and he certainly wasn't laughing."

"No-one said 'Best foot forward' but we were tempted," continues Mimi, trying her best to lighten things for young Jane, who was as white as snot.

"We could all do with a stiff drink," says Jack.

"Instead of a stiff," says Robbie.

"The police are on their way," announces Greaty. "In the meantime, we mustn't touch anything and no-one is to go anywhere near the body. Nobody can leave, either. We just have to wait for the D.I to arrive. She said we should turn our phones off, and I explained to her that we would have done that anyway as we were going to be rehearsing, so no-one at home would be surprised if they couldn't get hold of us."

"Whoops," I say. "I've already phoned Tom and he's on his way. Sorry – I wasn't thinking straight."

"No-one else should do that," insists Greaty, looking daggers at me. "The police don't want the scene to be over-run with extra people. Obviously." Again, he looks at me as if I'm a noodle. Which I am, I suppose. Still, I'm really glad when my Tom walks in. My knight in shining ardour.

Chapter 10

D.I. Jones looks very smart, in both senses of the word. There's a keen intelligence shining out of those designer-bespectacled eyes, and the trouser suit skims the surface of her slim body without emphasising the curves that are undoubtedly there underneath. A neat blonde bob softens her strong jawline, but there's nothing else soft about her. Jack had expressed doubts about having a woman D.I. in charge, but he's almost saluting when he sees her. We're in good hands, I think. She's got a poppet of a constable with her. Honestly, he looks about twelve. Big Bambi eyes and sticky-out ears – and he seems as nervous as a rabbi, so it's probably his first murder as well as ours.

"My name's Grace Jones and this is Constable Ben Laing. My forensic team will go straight through to the crime scene while I get some primary information from you. I'll try not to keep you for too long tonight but I shall be conducting in-depth interviews from tomorrow onwards. As no doubt you are aware from watching T.V. dramas, it is customary to set up an Incident Room in the local police station. Unfortunately, the police station in Middle Pidding was closed down a few years ago and has now, I believe, been converted to what is called a Des Res. Your nearest station is over at Ayrton."

"Does that mean we'll have to slog over there to be interviewed? Most of us run businesses here in Pidding. It really will make life very awkward if we have to spend a couple of hours every time you want to question us," says Bunty politely but forcefully. Everyone hurries to agree with her.

"And I'm the District Nurse, with a full agenda of care every day," adds Mimi importantly.

"Believe me," replies Grace Jones, "it's just as inconvenient for me. The only other thing that I could authorise is setting up a crime scene centre here in the village if we can find a suitable place. I would have suggested that here at the Village Hall might be possible, but of course there's a crime scene at the back of it."

"Well, you couldn't use it anyway," interposes Greaty apologetically. "You see, this is our only community centre, so every day there are playgroups and senior citizens' activities taking place in this hall, as well as a Pantomime every evening at the moment."

"No additional rooms?"

"No. Just the hall and the kitchen, I'm afraid."

"That's extremely inconvenient. I don't know the layout of the village so perhaps you can suggest another venue. Otherwise, it will have to be Ayrton."

We all put our thinking craps on. Robbie suggests the darts room at his pub, Leela offers her shop basement, newly decorated, several front rooms are put forward, but nothing seems to please Grace. Just as it looks as though it will have to be bloody Walmsley Ayrton, Tom steps forward with an idea. Bless.

"My wife's coffee shop is a double-fronted affair," he says. "We could screen off one side for you, and Jenny could carry on working in the other half. It's in the heart of the village with the added advantage that you would have coffee and refreshments on tap and you could use my office equipment in the room above. I run an insurance agency over the shop, you see."

"'er cakes are bloody marvellous," adds Jack, as if that would be enough to tip the balance. And who knows, perhaps it is, because Grace Jones agrees that it's worth a try. I'm as happy as a sandbag about it because I'll be able to keep tabs on everything. I've got a feeling my knowledge of the villagers will prove invaluable to Miss Jones. Tom dashes off to re-arrange my shop straight away so that Grace can start on time in the morning.

"Ben will come round taking your names, addresses and mobile numbers while I speak to the people who discovered the body. If we can ascertain the plain facts tonight, that will be sufficient. Tomorrow we shall know more about the cause and time of death and then I shall interview everyone in more depth. So try to relax and do your best to think clearly about tonight's events."

I hand over another of my trusty cast lists to young Ben while Grace Jones singles out Goody and Jane as the discoverers. Goody is flustered and Jane is petrified, but Grace manages to calm them down enough to give her the 'plain facts'.

"I needed to go to the loo. Before starting to interview people," explains Jane fitfully. "I'm a reporter, you see. For the local paper. Writing an article about the panto. 'Cinderella'."

"I'm the Stage Manager so Greatorex, the Director, asked me to show Jane to the toilets. She went in and I was about to come back to the hall when she screamed. I followed her inside and there was Bertram on the floor looking awful."

"We ran back to the hall. Then Mrs Merry and Mrs Beaufort went to check that he was really dead. Then Greatorex rang the police."

Grace nods and congratulates them on being clear and succinct. She turns to Mimi and Bunty: "So four of you went into the toilet area? It's a good job there was no blood to trample around. Did either of you touch the body?"

Mimi bristles a bit at the underlying criticism and tells her that there was absolutely no need to touch the body as it was perfectly obvious that Bertram was deceased.

"I suspect I've seen far more dead bodies than you, Miss Jones, in my years as a fully-trained medico. There's no need to fear that anything was trampled on," she said haughtily.

"Except a couple of bees," added Bunty.

"I beg your pardon? Did you say bees?"

"She asked bitingly," quips Robbie.

"Yes, bees," replies Bunty. "There were several dead bees on the floor."

"How curious."

"Hang on a minute," says Leela. "The thing is, Bertram was allergic, just like me. I'm wondering if he might have been stung by a bee in there and died because of it. That would make his death just an accident and not murder, wouldn't it?"

"We shall certainly look into that," Grace assures us. "Now before I let you go, I would just like you to tell us when you last saw Bertram. Shall we start with you, Mr Manston?"

"Yesterday evening at rehearsal. Although I did bump into him this morning by the library. I was on my way to the building site. I think he was going into the pharmacy," says Greaty. "Is that right, Bunty?"

"Yes, he did come in this morning to buy some travel sickness pills," affirms Bunty.

"Was he planning a holiday?" asks Grace.

Robbie is quick to say, "Not that he told me! He hadn't booked any time off, I can tell you. Mind you, he was a bit of a mystery."

"When did you last see him, Mr Slack?" asks Grace.

"He was working in the pub last night and then he was here rehearsing. That's it. He had today off."

"I don't think last night's rehearsal is relevant here. I'm interested to find out who saw him earlier today."

Tony steps up to the plate and tells her that Bertram had gone into his Off Licence at about 3.30 to buy a bottle of wine. Then Jack says he saw him later in the afternoon at about 4 up at the site and then a bit later in the village.

"I was walking to the pub for a drink and a bite to eat. He was in the pub car park and he called me over," explains Jack.

"What for?" enquires Grace.

"Nothing significant. He just wanted to remind me about the meeting with Jane Makepeace before the rehearsal tonight."

"So what time was that?"

"About five o'clock. He then drove off up the High Street in the direction of the theatre."

Mimi then puts in her halfpenny worth, telling us all that she saw him in the car park at about 4.30, obviously just before Jack.

"I was about to visit a patient when I saw him. We had a little chat –nothing in particular, just lovely weather sort of thing."

"I saw him too," pipes up Goody. "I was coming out of the Co-op with biscuits for tonight. He was outside Wendy's shop."

Wendy confirms this: "He popped his head round the door to say hello."

"What about you, Leela? Any sightings today?"

"Indeed. He came into my shop at about three. He bought himself a buttonhole, a lovely little yellow rosebud. I must admit I wondered what the special occasion was, but I didn't ask."

"Makes a change," mutters Jack.

No-one else volunteers any information about today. The rest of us hadn't seen him since last night's rehearsal, except Chris and Freddy who hadn't seen him since the day before that and young Jane who hadn't seen him at all.

"So that makes the latest sighting at about 5 o'clock. Nothing after that?" asks Grace.

We're all shaking our heads, though we all know that SOMEBODY saw him after that. I hope it wasn't one of us!

"Thank you all. P.C. Laing has got your numbers and we'll start interviewing tomorrow morning at ten o'clock. I'd like to know a bit about your relationship with Bertram, just to help me paint a fuller picture of him. Shall we start with you, Jenny, as you'll be there anyway?"

"Could you see me a bit later? Breakfast and elevenses are busy times for the shop. There's a real lull between two and three, if that would be convenient for you?"

Grace smiles – she's got a lovely smile – and says that would be fine. Wendy puts her hand up tentatively, as if she's back in school, and she volunteers to go first as she needn't open up her shop until later.

"A last word before you go home," says Grace. "There's no way of preventing news of the death spreading to the community but I must stress the importance of your not saying a word about what you've seen and heard here tonight. We don't yet know what's important, and gossip about the circumstances might warn the perpetrator. I know you will all be anxious to find out what happened to your friend and the best way you can help us do that is to keep your mouths shut."

Duly chastened, we all trot off to our homes, avid to tell our nearest and dearest all about it! Tom has already screened off half the shop and is just re-arranging tables and chairs. I notice that he's put a nice big table for Grace Jones with two chairs on each side. It's a proper little interrogation room.

"That's brilliant, love," I enthuse as I give him a well-deserved cuddle. As we stand there, we realise that we're on full view to the nation. That doesn't bother us, of course, but Grace and Ben won't want the nosey eyes of Middle Pidding watching their every move.

"Have we got any spare curtains?" asks Tom. "I could string something across to give them a bit of privacy."

"Our dining room ones would fit. Actually, it's time we had some new ones – I've seen some lovely material in Wendy's. Every cloud has a silver shining, doesn't it?"

Tom smiles. "I love the way you mangle sayings."

I don't know what he means! Well, yes I do. Little does he know that I sometimes do it on purpose to entertain him. My old mum used to say that husbands never stray if there's laughter at home, and the same goes for wives. I love Tom's puns and he obviously laughs at my sayings.

"Do you mind if we don't take down the curtains tonight? I'm bushed. We'll get up early tomorrow and do it," pleads Tom.

"May flocks of angels sing thee to thy chest," I say.

Chapter 11

Did you know there are two six o'clocks every day? I'm familiar with the yard-arm one, but that other one while the world is still in darkness is a new one on me. I don't like it much. But needs must when the devil jives. I'm rather glad the neighbours don't see me balancing on top of the stepladder unfastening all those wretched things that hold curtains in place. The air is blue and it isn't all dust. It's Tom's idea to get all the hard physical work done before we have breakfast, so here we are now at the coffee shop putting a curtain barrier up between bookers and lookers.

"The villagers will never forgive me for this," I sigh.

"Course they will. I bet you'll have a full half-shop instead of a half-full shop. Mrs Trundle will have her hearing aid up to full volume and they'll all be fighting over the tables nearest the partition."

"I thought it was a great idea to have the Incident Room here until I realised that having customers all the time will mean that I can't hear the interviews. If we're going to solve this murder, Tom, we need to be fully in the know."

"Oh, so we're solving the murder, are we?" laughed Tom. "I thought we were just fulfilling our civic duty."

"Rubbish. You're just as keen as I am. Any thoughts so far?"

"My thoughts centre around a milky coffee and a couple of pain au raisins. I can't deliberate on an empty tum."

We have a big freezer full of all the necessaries so it didn't matter that we couldn't do our usual baking last night. We tuck into our breakfasts sitting behind the counter so that we don't make a mess in either half of the shop. It's very cosy and warm and we almost forget why we're doing it. Tom is obviously chewing over a problem as well as his raisins.

"I think I might take a couple of days off from the office. How would it be if I was here in the shop with you, doing most of the serving, so you could keep an ear open for developments?" he says.

"I knew you'd come up with a plan!" I chortle. (Yes, that is a word and it sums up all the glee in my voice, so there!) "I could station myself at the Hail Mary end of the counter."

"The what?"

"The 'Hail Mary, full of **Grace**' end," I say, which makes him laugh. "I'll keep busy prepping food and hoping Grace doesn't catch on that my ears are flapping all the time."

"We haven't got anything to go on yet, except that Bertram was last seen at about 5 o'clock heading towards the theatre," muses Tom.

"Wearing a buttonhole," I add.

"As if he was celebrating something. It wasn't his birthday, was it?"

"Definitely not. Don't you remember? It falls on April Fool's Day, as Robbie would never let him forget. Maybe it's someone else's birthday, but if it was a member of the cast I'm sure something would have been said. No, that's mystery number one to be solved."

There's an insistent tapping on the door and we can see Grace and Ben out there. It's half past nine and they'll want to be settled in before Wendy comes in at ten. Tom proudly shows them their quarters (well, halves) and they seem pleased with the arrangements. They just have time to tell us that Bertram's death occurred between five and seven, and that it was definitely a poisoning, before Wendy is hovering on the doorstep, early and nervous. Grace is sensitive enough to see that Wendy's in a bit of a state and she asks me to get a round of coffee for herself, Ben and Wendy. That was nice of her, I think, and she goes up in my estimation. When they're settled, Grace starts off with surface facts – you know, name and address and occupation, even though Ben took all that down last night. Wendy's voice starts as a whisper but gradually reaches normal volume as she gets more confident.

"Now, Miss Cotton, you said last night that Bertram popped his head round the door yesterday morning. Does he usually do that?" asks Grace.

"No, not really," Wendy replies, gazing into her coffee cup as if she would find an answer there. "I suppose it was more than just a passing wave."

"What was it then?"

"He wanted a deposit for the work he's going to do on my basement room. I just handed him the £10 in an envelope and he said he'd start on it next week."

She suddenly starts crying, that hiccuppy sort of crying you get when it takes you by surprise. She must be realising that he won't be around to do the work now.

"My basement. It's got to be done. It's the aluminium. Who can I get now?" she sobs. "It could get on my fabrics. Dangerous. All that stock wasted. Who can I get?"

Grace Jones obviously can't care less who she is going to get, but she's polite enough to reassure Wendy that there are plenty of builders around. But I'm puzzled. Wendy is an expert in her own limited field, but her knowledge of the world leaves a lot to be desired. Why on earth should she think that aluminium is dangerous? Suddenly, I know. I scribble a note to Grace and take it to her under the guise of giving them a plate of biscuits. The note says: Not aluminium. Asbestos!"

"The important thing here is to concentrate on Bertram, isn't it?" Grace is saying. "Did he say anything else to you? Did you see him again?"

Wendy shakes her head vigourously, still mopping up tears. Then Grace obviously reads the note and looks over to my corner. She nods that she's understood.

"I think you may mean that your basement has asbestos in it, Wendy. Is that right?" she asks.

"That's what I said. It's dangerous, isn't it?"

"Indeed it is. Does Bertram have a licence to remove it? Was that the job he was going to do for you?" Grace queries, looking concerned.

"It had to be covered up, you see. Battens and expensive plasterboard instead of a quick coat of emulsion. Just like Leela's," explains Wendy fretfully.

Ben and Grace exchange meaningful looks. They know as well as I do that you have to have asbestos removed by a licensed firm because of the danger to the public. Our local primary school was shut up over the whole summer holiday a couple of years ago because it was found round the lagging of the hot water pipes. It sounds to me as if our Bertram was doing a cover-up job. Was that illegal? Ben is making a note of it before they move on.

"Can I ask what time you got to the Village Hall that evening?" asks Grace.

"I locked up my shop just as Robbie was leaving his pub so we walked to the Hall together. That would have been at 6.30 and we got to the Hall at about quarter to seven. You can check that with Robbie."

"Yes, we will do that. Do you have any ideas as to who might have had a grudge against Bertram? Looking out of your shop window, I expect you see all the comings and goings. And people probably chat to you while you fit their costumes. Any bits of chatter that might be helpful?" asks Grace.

"Not really. He seemed pretty happy recently."

"Well, thank you for your time, Miss Cotton. Off you go – and don't worry about your basement."

When Wendy has fluttered her way out, Grace and Ben whisper about asbestos for a bit. I hope they noticed that Wendy inadvertently dropped our Leela in it when she talked about the job being just what Leela had had done. If Leela knew that the job was illegal, could Bertram have been blackmailing her? If someone buying her shop were to find out, there'd be all sorts of trouble. My mind is going ten to the doesn't.

Grace then asks Ben who he thinks should be questioned next. He sensibly proposes Robbie, so they can check Wendy's and his arrival time at the theatre. Grace looks pleased with his suggestion. I'm getting the feeling that Ben Laing may be a very new constable and she's training him a bit. He's on the phone immediately to Robbie, and I notice that Tom is doing a sterling job shepherding customers to their seats and taking orders as if he was born to it. I'm going to dash to the loo so I don't miss any of Robbie's words.

I get back just as Robbie arrives. He signals to Tom that he wants a black coffee and Ben ushers him in to Grace.

"I hope we can make this quick," says Robbie brusquely. "Pubs don't run themselves."

"The speed of the interview relies entirely on the fullness of your answers, Mr Slack. Shall we begin?"

There's a touch of steel there, I think to myself. This lady's not for gurning. I take the coffee over to Robbie, making myself as small and inconspicuous as possible, and I creep back behind my arras.

"Now, Mr Slack, you said that Bertram had the day off yesterday. Does that mean that you didn't see him at all?"

"I forgot that he came in to pick up some wages he was owed. I think that was round about four o'clock but I can't be more precise than that," says Robbie gruffly.

"Was it before five?" asks Ben.

"Oh yes, definitely. He was wearing a stupid flower in his buttonhole and smirking all over his face. I mean, who wears buttonholes? It just looked silly, as if he was off to get married or something. He didn't stop to chat, just collected his money and left."

"What time did you arrive at the Hall last night?"

"I can be precise about that. I grabbed a quick pie behind the bar and set off at 6.30. Wendy was just locking up her shop so I escorted her to the theatre. We arrived at precisely 6.45."

"Excellent. Thank you. As you worked alongside Bertram, I expect you got to know him quite well. Are you aware of any problems he might have had? Anybody who might have had a grudge against him?" asks Grace.

"Nothing that I know of. Mind you, he was a grumpy sod and a bit of a nosey parker. I caught him looking at the pub's receipts last week and I told him to keep his nose out. He was always asking questions about how to run a pub and I got the feeling he was trying to learn the tricks of the trade so he could become a landlord himself some day."

"Did that bother you?"

"Not unless he had his eyes on MY pub. I'd be furious if that was on his mind. But I think he was just nosy. Anyway, he seemed much happier over the past few months so I can't pinpoint anything for you. Sorry and all that."

"Was he married?" blurts out Ben. "Or, I mean, in a relationship?"

"Not him. He had a room above the pub and he sometimes brought a young lady back with him. But no-one in particular. I don't think you'll find an angry woman at the back of all this."

"Thank you, Mr Slack. You can return to your pub now."

"It's a nightmare right now. I've got to replace Bertram and find someone to cover for me while we're performing the panto. My poor wife, Alice, is tearing her hair out trying to work the bar, cook the food and phone the agencies for replacements. Bloody nightmare."

"Surely the pantomime won't be going on, will it?" asks Grace curiously.

"As far as I know, Greaty's going to step into the role of the second Ugly Sister."

Well, that's news to me. Greaty will hate being a
Dame but I suppose that will be his only alternative.
At least he knows all the moves and the business.
The show must go on and all that. On with the
Muttley!

When Robbie goes, Grace and Ben have a conflab
about who to call in next so I take them a cup of
coffee and ask if they want a snack. Ben's about to
say yes, but Grace just gives him one of those looks
and he subsides. Poor lad, he needs a bit of feeding
up.

"Did you know that the panto is going ahead?"
Grace asks me.

"Me? No. I haven't heard anything. You'll have to
ask Greaty himself – or Goody," I reply.

Just then, Tom comes round the screen to say that
Tony Cropper has arrived in a right state, insisting
on seeing the police immediately. We all look at
each other in a puzzled but interested way and
Grace tells Tom to show him through. I hurry back
to my corner as he arrives.

"Titty's gone! She wasn't at home last night – I
thought she might have heard the murder news and
gone to stay with her mother, but when I phoned

this morning, her mum knew nothing about it. Has she been here to see you?"

"No, Mr Cropper. We haven't seen her. Please sit down, you look upset. Ben, go and get a coffee for Mr Cropper – and bring the sugar bowl."

That's a turn-up for the crook. Maybe Titania's done a runner! Does that mean she's the killer? I can't believe that, not our Titty. I could believe she's walked out on Tony, though. My hands are shaking as I hand the coffee cup over to Ben, and his are just as shaky taking it. He forgets the sugar so he has to come back and he's as white as a sweet.

"Actually, Mr Cropper, our forensic team found a note addressed to you stuck to the mirror in the theatre toilet. It's been dusted for fingerprints, unsuccessfully, so I can give it to you. It may provide some answers."

Tony grabs the envelope as if it were a lifeline and rips out the note. His mouth hangs open as he reads - not an attractive sight – and I'm literally holding my breath. He reaches the end, shakes his head, and goes back to the beginning.

"Would you mind sharing it with us, Mr Cropper?"

I'm pretty certain they've read it already but I suppose they want to make sure he's taken in whatever it says.

"She's done a runner. Left me," he says blankly.

"Would you read it out for us?"

"She says: 'It was bound to happen, Tony. We've been unhappy for a long time now. I'm running away with Bertram. We've been in love for a year now, ever since we were Tweedledum and Tweedledee in last year's Alice in Wonderland. We had so many extra rehearsals to make sure our lines were exactly in unison that we got closer and closer. Becoming bridge partners when you left the club was the icing on the cake. So that's it. Bertram is going to stick this note on the mirror in the loo and Goody's going to make sure you see it. By the time you read it, we'll be on our way to Gretna Green. I'm going on ahead and Bertram will catch a later train. We'll soon be man and wife. I don't think we'll ever be back, but you never know. I told Goody we'd return but that was just to stop her crying. Goodbye and good riddance.

Your never-wife

Titania

P.S. I bet you wish we'd got married instead of just pretending. Serves you right for not committing!'"

Poor bloke, he looks completely shocked. I nearly drop the coffee jar when she says about not being married. That's a complete surprise. Tony was no great shakes as a partner, but I'm not sure Bertram would have been much better. It might be a case of marry in haste, repent at Leicester.

Grace breaks the silence. "I take it you didn't know about this, Mr Cropper."

"Course not. If I'd known, I wouldn't have let it happen," replies Tony through gritted teeth.

"Perhaps you found out and decided to kill Bertram," suggests Ben.

"Don't be stupid. If I'd found out, I'd have killed **her** not him!"

"Now there's a pleasant thought," says Grace sarcastically. "Is there anyone else on your hit list?"

"Goody Gofer has got a lot to answer for. The letter says she knew all about it. I hope you'll give her a good going-over."

"We shall certainly be questioning her."

"And bring back that cow Titty, wherever she is. Bloody Gretna Green, I ask you. Anyone would think she was a sixteen-year-old."

"Let us have her mobile number, Mr Cropper, and we'll see that she gets the full information."

"Maybe she did him in herself and then ran away. Maybe he was going to ditch her," accuses Tony.

You could see that he was clutching at strawbs, poor bloke. Anything to divert suspicion from himself. Because you have to admit, he must be the Prime Suspect now. If anyone tried to run off with my Tom, they'd get no mercy from me. Mind you, Tony and Titty didn't have our sort of relationship. I don't blame Titty for trying to get away. Tom calls me over to sort out Mrs Widdecombe's bill – she always has two cups and tries to pay for one. By the time I get back in my corner, the interview has moved on.

"So the only people you think might have had a grudge against Bertram are some customers who weren't entirely pleased with their burglar alarms? Rather a puny motive for murder, wouldn't you say?" says Grace.

"Leela wasn't too happy about his work on her shop, moaning about it being very expensive," offers Tony, scraping the barrel.

"Really?" scoffs Ben.

Suddenly, Tony sits upright in his chair and looks as though he's had an electric shock. He scrabbles in his pocket for his phone.

"I've just thought. The bank account! Surely she can't have …"

Grace and Ben share a glance and watch Tony frantically pressing buttons to get his account balance. They don't have to wait long.

"No!" shouts Tony, and every head in the other half of the shop perks up as every ear gets pointed towards the partition like radar. You could hear a pin plop.

"Cow! She's emptied it. All the holiday money. She's left me with fifty quid and skedaddled with the rest."

I still don't like him much but I do feel sorry for him right now, losing his wife and his money all at once. It's like that bloke in 'The Merchant of Venice', isn't it? "My ducats, my daughter, but oh my ducats!" I think Tony probably cares more about the money as well. It seems to me that his outrage is genuine so maybe that proves he's innocent of the murder. Mind you, he still might have done it without knowing that Titty had taken the cash. So now he's on his way back to the Offy, threatening all sorts against Titty when and if she's found. Grace and Ben must be thinking that the plot is thickening a bit too much. They've got to set in motion a search for Titania Cropper as well as solving the murder of her lover.

Chapter 12

Young Ben sidles up to the counter and his puppydog eyes slide to the array of cakes and goodies. He might just as well have a sign round his neck saying 'Feed Me'. I cut him a slab of gingerbread and he eats it surreptitiously while he's waiting for me to make their coffee. I take as long as I can so he doesn't get indigestion. When he carries the cups back to Grace, I can see her noticing a couple of stray crumbs on his chin and I'm waiting for fireworks. However, she just does a sort of secret smile and gives me a wink. I'm liking her more and more.

"I think we need to interview Goody Gofer next, don't you, Ben?" says Grace.

"Yes, definitely," he replies sagely. "She certainly knows more about all this than she let on last night. I'll phone her to come in now."

When he's done that, Grace continues: "The letter says that Goody had undertaken to make sure that Tony saw the letter. It could mean that Bertram actually gave it to her – in which case she would have been the last person to see him alive."

"Or maybe she killed him," suggests Ben excitedly.

"Motive?" asks Grace doubtfully.

"Mmm. She was upset that her friend Titania was leaving…"

"That's rather a flimsy reason, but we'll see what she has to say for herself. While we're waiting, I think we could have some food. We need to keep our strength up. Come on, let's see what's on offer."

Young Ben beams from 'ere to 'ere as the prospect of yet more cake fills him with delight. They come out to look at the possibilities, which makes every customer concentrate hurriedly on their own tables as if they have no interest whatever in what's going on in purdah. If Greaty could see the brilliant acting going on, he'd never worry about casting again. Tom serves Ben first with another slab of gingerbread – and I notice that he's put a piece under the counter for himself, the sly old fox. Grace is still deliberating as I make the coffee, but eventually goes for carrot cake. I wonder if I should tell her that the sultanas I put into it are soaked in whiskey, but I decide not to. Too many cooks spoil the breath. They take their little repasts back behind the iron curtain and I follow them up with serviettes.

As I emerge, Goody hurries in looking grey with worry. I tell her that D.I. Jones is just sending off some memos and I suggest she might like a coffee while she's waiting. She jumps at it, poor thing. She often has decaf, but today she opts for full strength plus a heaped teaspoon of sugar. I sit down with her and try to calm her down a bit. Watching her shred a serviette is doing my head in.

"I heard that Greaty is going ahead with the panto," I say. "Is that right?"

"Yes. Well, he's going to try. If he plays the other Ugly Sister, he thinks we can manage."

"Who'll play the front end of the horse?" I ask provocatively.

She looks like the proverbial rabbit in the headlines.

"Do people know?" she whispers.

"If by people you mean the police, then yes, dear, they do."

"Oh dear. Was it the letter?"

"Yes, of course. You'd best come clean when you talk to them," I advise her, and she nods despairingly.

I see Ben giving the plates and cups back to Tom before he comes over to get Goody. She's trembling too much to carry her coffee so he picks up her cup for her. It's nice to see kindness in a copper. Back I go to my little hidey hole.

"Miss Gofer, it has come to our notice that you were cognisant of a particular covert relationship. Would you mind telling us about your involvement?" says Grace formally. Her tone is enough to scare the bejesus out of anyone. Goody can see that she can't prevaricate.

"Titania is my best friend. All I did was help her be happy. No-one could have foreseen that it would end so tragically."

"You'd better start at the beginning. How long have you known about the affair?"

"I've always known that she and Tony were washed up. I could never understand why she stayed with him, especially as they weren't legally married," sighs Goody.

"Oh, you knew about that, too?"

"Yes. Her telling me about it was what really sealed our friendship. She trusted me absolutely, you see, so I gave the same loyalty back to her. We told each other everything. She was afraid of leaving Tony but when she fell in love with Bertram she had the possibility of escaping. It was all carefully planned. She went home from the Offy with a pretend migraine and left on an early train to St. Pancras. Bertram was supposed to leave a goodbye letter in the theatre loo and catch a later train, meeting her in London. I promised I'd make sure that Tony saw the note when we were all at the rehearsal that evening."

"Why didn't they go off together?" asks Ben.

"Good question," agrees Grace, smiling at her young apprentice.

"Yes, I thought it would have been more romantic to run away together. But Titty was so afraid that someone would see them with each other and report back to Tony. They wanted to be well away before he found out. Once they were married, she would feel safe," explains Goody, dabbing her eyes with the remains of her serviette.

"So, did you see Bertram at the theatre when he left the note?"

"Oh no. I wasn't there. I just had to ensure that the note got to Tony that evening. In fact, I kept myself very busy all day just to stop myself from thinking about it. I typed some letters for Greaty in the morning and took them to the site for him to sign at about two. Then I went to the Post Office at about three for stamps as I'd run out. You can check with them. Oh, and before that I went for some biscuits and milk to the Co-op. No, no, sorry – I went there AFTER the Post Office, so at about three thirty to four. I popped back to the building site after four to remind Jack about the meeting with the reporter Jane Whatsit, then I went home to change for the meeting. I was dashing from pillar to post."

"Can anyone confirm that you were at home after going to Mr Manston's building site to see Jack?" asks Grace.

"I don't think so. Oh dear. Wait, did I have any phone calls? Can't remember. Let me just check my mobile. Ah yes, Titania phoned me at 4.23. How precise these things are! We talked for ten minutes, it says. I phoned Greaty at 5.10 to tell him I'd got the milk and biscuits and was on my way to his place, and it says we talked for three minutes, 5.10 until 5.13. I got to Greaty's at 5.30."

"What was Titania's phone call about?"

"She told me she was really happy and that I mustn't forget to make sure that Tony saw the note. Oh dear…"

"You'll miss her, won't you?" says Grace gently.

"I will. She told me she would come back, but I honestly doubted that she would. I couldn't imagine Titty and Bertram living in the same village as Tony. But I knew she would let me know where they ended up and then I could visit – and we'd always go on talking on the phone."

"Speaking of which, have you heard from Titania today? She must have been puzzled when Bertram didn't turn up."

That opens the floodgates. The serviette remnants are useless and it's a good job that Grace is equipped with a box of man-size tissues. Goody is sobbing her heart out, poor lamb. My instinct is to run over to her but I'm holding myself back. I don't want Grace to realise that I'm listening to every word. Ben is looking embarrassed at the sight of so much female emotion, and I think Grace is trying to work out the reason for such a lot of grief. Does she think Goody is conscience-stricken? We're all waiting for the tornado to pass.

"I'm sorry," Goody hiccups, "I feel so guilty about all this. If I hadn't encouraged Titty in the first place, if I'd told her to be more open with Tony, maybe this wouldn't have happened. And worst of all, I didn't tell her last night about Bertram's murder. I just couldn't. I've ignored her calls this morning, too. I just can't tell her. I've left it to the police. I'm such a coward. I'm so ashamed of myself. Will she ever forgive me?"

She's off again, weeping like a willow. Brother Jack will have to build us an ark soon. I must say I'm rather shocked that she's left Titty high and dry. I would have thought that her first concern would have been to comfort her friend, but I suppose it's difficult to give such news over the phone. Maybe it will be best broken to her by a sensitive policewoman, then Goody can be there with open arms when Titty gets back to the village. I'm assuming she'll have to come back here, anyway.

"The London police have already contacted her at the St Pancras hotel and they are making arrangements to bring her back. We'll have to question her, of course, but after that I'm sure you will want to see her and commiserate with her," says Grace.

"Oh yes. She'll be able to stay with me. She may need protection from Tony, though."

"She will get everything she needs from us, don't worry."

"Poor Titty," sighs Goody. "This should have been the first day of the rest of her life."

"It still is," states Grace pragmatically. "It's just not the life she was expecting."

They all nod philosophically and Grace brings the interview to a close. Everyone needs a break. I usually stay open all through the lunch period, but today I just can't face it. We put up the CLOSED sign and persuade everyone to sup up and go home. We invite Grace and Ben to join us for a light lunch, not thinking for a moment that they'll agree, but they're eager to do so. You could have knocked me down with a feature. So it's sausage rolls and coleslaw all round with elderflower pressé. Tom manages to indicate that we ought to bring out Bertram's notebook so I fetch it from my bag behind the counter.

"Bertram dropped this in the shop recently," I say, handing the book to Grace. "I kept forgetting to give it back to him. We did have a little look inside, and there's one particular page you should examine, because it's really strange."

I point out our puzzle page and we can see that it baffles them just as much as it does us.

"We thought the letters might be people's initials, but we don't have any Xs in the village," says Tom.

"X marks the spot!" says Ben with a beaming smile, but a glare from Grace makes him see the inanity of the remark. I'm beginning to wonder how many brain cells are lurking under that smart haircut, but his next comment has me riveted.

"X always means ten to me," he says. "Roman numerals."

Tom almost snatches the book away from Grace. "By heck, that might be it!" He puts the page on the table so we can all see and proceeds to point out that the first column that has an X at the top has three ticks underneath and 30 at the bottom. That could mean that J (whoever that is) paid three lots of £10. Then LX and WX had two ticks and totals of £20.

"If that's right," I say excitedly, "this could be a record of Bertram getting money from people. I mean blackmail!"

"Extortion," chorus Tom, Grace and Ben.

And it's at this point that Ben blows my socks off when he says, "So L is 50, D is 500 and C is 100. Pounds, I mean."

We look again and we can see that it all adds up. Grace glances at Ben as if she's wondering if she had underestimated him until now. He's looking as pleased as lunch.

"Does that indicate that the first letter is a name and the second letter is the amount they're paying out?" I ask.

"That makes sense," says Tom. "So can we work out who they are?"

Grace doesn't seem to mind us chiming in on her investigation so we concentrate on the first letters.

"M could be Mimi. G could be Goody," I say.

"Or Greatorex," cautions Grace. "In fact, if it's a payment of £500, maybe it's more likely to be Greatorex."

"J could be Jack, L could be Leela, W is Wendy and R is Robbie."

"That leaves E. No-one in the cast has a name beginning with E," I point out, which deflates us all a bit.

"Of course there is," says a triumphant Tom. "Bunty's real name is Elizabeth!"

We all sit back, really pleased with ourselves.

"So," says Grace, "it looks as though Bertram had a little blackmail racket going."

"Extortion," we all chorus.

"Unfortunately, that gives us motives a-plenty. In fact, it looks as though nearly everyone had reason to hate Bertram. Now we have to find which motive was strong enough to lead to murder."

Chapter 13

Ben had arranged for Greaty to come in after lunch for his little tête-a-tête and when he arrives we open up the shop for business again. There are a few disgruntled customers who had wanted to come in while we were temporarily closed but they forgive us when they realise they haven't missed anything. Greaty waves away the offer of a coffee in his best haughty manner and urges Grace to "extricate her finger" and get on with it as he has so much to do to save the panto, as if a panto matters compared with solving a murder, but there's none so blind as those who will not seek.

"Mr Manston, I believe you said your last sighting of Bertram was when you bumped into him yesterday morning. Is that correct?" asks Grace, as cool as a newcomer.

"Actually, I remembered later that he popped over to the building site in the early afternoon, just before Goody arrived with some papers for me to sign at about two o'clock."

"Why was that?"

"I've no idea. We had nothing to talk about and I was pretty busy. I got the feeling that he was just filling in time. He had the day off, apparently, so maybe he just didn't want to go back to his cheap little room at the pub."

"What were your movements after that?" asks Ben.

"I was on site all afternoon. We stopped working at five and I dashed home to change and tidy the house before that silly little reporter was going to come. Goody phoned to let me know she was on her way and she arrived at 5.30 with the tea stuff, so we were ready by 6 o'clock when Jane arrived. We all made some awkward small talk until we set off for the theatre."

"Awkward?" asks Grace innocently.

"Oh for heaven's sake. Everyone knows about her vicious rumour-mongering when my company was converting the old chemical site. I lost a lot of money through her. She had absolutely no proof that I was involved in the chemical dumping but that didn't stop her from writing rabid articles about my supposed culpability. She did just the same to poor old Jack as well. I nearly refused to let her do the crit on the panto but Goody persuaded me that the publicity was worth an hour or two of discomfort."

"I presume you'll have to cancel now, though," says Ben.

"Not a bit of it, dear boy. I shall step up to the plate and play the second Ugly. I can't let the cast down. They'll look to me to show the way. They've given six months of their lives to this, you know."

"Who'll play the horse?" queries Grace.

"Tony and Titty, of course," he replies.

"Ah, so you haven't heard. I thought the village rumour mill would have worked its magic by now."

Greaty looks from one to the other, trying to work out if they're crazy or just teasing him. His fingers are drumming on the table in an impatient rhythm until he can't contain his curiosity any longer and bursts out: "What? What haven't I heard?"

"Titty was running away with Bertram and is now in London, waiting pointlessly for him to arrive. She won't be here to be the Horse. Even if we got her back in time for the performance, I can't see Tony and her inhabiting the same costume, can you?" explains Grace.

Have you ever watched a balloon deflate? That's just what Greaty looks like. Mind you, he's "an actor, darling" so perhaps he's giving the performance of his life. He's sitting there looking dumbfounded, though, and I can see his eyes screwing up in concentration, trying to see a way out of the mess.

"The selfish bastards," he hisses. "How can they do this to their friends?"

"I'm truly sorry, Greatorex," says Grace, and I really think she is.

"Goody will have to take on the Horse," he announces. "She knows all the business. And Jenny will have to step up to Stage Manager."

He now has a triumphant look on his face, thinking he's solved the problems satisfactorily. He's completely forgotten about the murder, as if it was a minor incident whose significance was only that it affected the panto. In his mind, everyone will do what he tells them. A little humility wouldn't come amiss – I'm not sure I want to do stage management, thank you very much. Pride comes before a fault.

"With respect, Greatorex, I think you need to realise that a murder has taken place and that there's a murderer still at large. In all probability, it's one of your cast who is the perpetrator. When we find out who it is, there will be no possibility of 'the show must go on'. Perhaps you just have to bite the bullet now and cancel."

"I still believe it was some sort of accident," he replies haughtily. "I suggest you expedite your investigation as quickly as possible and put us all out of our misery. If there's nothing more, I shall bid you goodbye and get on with the arrangements that have to be made."

After he's swept out like the Demon King, Ben and Grace obviously don't know whether to laugh at his hubris or pity him. Grace gets a phone call from St Pancras saying that they have checked Titty's train ticket and can confirm that she was on the 3.55 train, so at least that rules her out as a suspect. One down, several to go.

Chapter 14

Mimi dashes in, followed closely by Bunty. Neither of them has been called but I suppose Mimi needs to put her patients first and fit us in when she has a break in her home visiting schedule. Grace agrees to see Mimi straight away and Bunty settles for a cup of coffee and a piece of Victoria Sponge while she's waiting for her turn. Tom chats to her while he's cutting a rather large piece of cake (I must warn him not to be over-generous or our profits will go down the train) and I get her coffee as quickly as I can. Meanwhile, Mimi is explaining that she's only got twenty minutes to spare.

"We'll be as speedy as possible, Mrs Merry. Now, I believe you said that you last saw Bertram at about 4.30 in the pub car park. It seems to be a strange place for you to be."

"Not at all. Did you think I was doing a bit of soliciting?" she laughs suggestively. "No, you see it's so central. I often park there and walk to clients' houses rather than trying to park in some of our narrow roads. That day, I had a short break before my next appointment so I was enjoying the luxury of just sitting."

"What did you and Bertram talk about?" asks Ben.

"Nothing much. The weather, the panto, the reporter coming that night. Really, nothing much. I remarked on the buttonhole he was wearing. He was looking smarter than usual, I thought. He said he was celebrating, but when I tried to delve a bit deeper he just tapped the side of his nose and said, "You'll see" or something like that. I had no idea at the time what that was all about, but frankly I wasn't really interested. Of course, I know now that he was running off with Titty. What a turn-up."

"You weren't giving him any money, then?"

"Why on earth would I be handing money over to Bertram? I'm not having any work done on my house."

She sounds very confident but I notice that her hand goes straight up to the amber necklace she's wearing, which I happen to know was a gift from one of her elderly patients. I must report that to Grace – it could be a reason for Bertram squeezing cash out of her. Since working on that list in Bertram's notebook, I've been trying to think of causes for blackmail from each of the possible people in the chart. Putting pressure on her patients

128

to 'remember her in their will' or to say thank you with a small gift would fit the bill.

"Can you think of anyone who might have had a grudge against Bertram?" asks Ben.

"I can't imagine that Tony was his best mate! If he knew about the affair, I mean. He's definitely got a brutal side to him, as Titty will tell you - if she comes back."

Grace's mobile rings and she takes the call straight away, so it must be from someone important. I take the opportunity to pass Bunty's coffee to Tom so he can serve her. I can't make much of Grace's side of the phone conversation, except that she's cross that she's only just been given a particular piece of information. I'm dying to know what it is, but she's saying nothing.

"Going on to the rehearsal evening, you and Mrs Beaufort went into the toilet area to check if Bertram was dead, didn't you? Tell me, did you see anything in there?" asks Grace.

"Apart from the blooming body, you mean? Well, let me think. There was an envelope stuck to the mirror but I didn't clock whose name was on it. Oh, and there were a few dead bees on the floor by the door. I can't think of anything else."

"Did you happen to see an epipen?" asks Grace.

"No. I would have noticed that, I assure you. I do know that Bertram was allergic to bee stings and my first thought on seeing his body was that it was anaphylactic shock but his face and tongue were so distorted that I ruled that out. The bees were definitely dead, anyway."

"Do you know if Bertram carried an epipen around with him?" pursued Grace.

"Of course he did. He was paranoid about bees. He went into a total panic if a bee came anywhere near him. He always had an epi in his pocket. There was always one in the First Aid box at the side of the stage, too, in case of an accident while he was in costume."

"I see. Well, thank you, Mrs Merry. That will be all for now. Please don't go far from the village in case we need to speak to you again."

"All my calls are local this afternoon. I'll be at the theatre tonight, I suppose, unless Greatorex cancels. I really hope he does. Most people think it's in very bad taste to carry on."

When she's gone, Grace turns to Ben with a really serious look on her face and tells him that there was an epipen found just underneath Bertram's body. She doesn't have time to tell him more because Bunty is putting her nose round the screen asking if she can be 'done' next so she can get back to the pharmacy.

"By all means, Mrs Beaufort. Come and sit down. We won't keep you long. Can we just check what you saw inside the toilet when you and Mrs Merry went to check on Bertram's body?" says Grace patiently.

"We could see he was dead straight away. It didn't look like a comfortable death either, if you see what I mean. That face has haunted my dreams," she shudders.

"Anything else? In the room?" adds Ben.

"Insects on the floor. Envelope on the mirror. Smell of urine where he'd wet himself," Bunty elaborates.

"Did you see an epipen?" asks Ben earnestly.

"Ah, you're wondering if he was stung by one of those dratted bees, aren't you? I really don't think so. The bees were mere husks, very old and dried out. I noticed a prop beehive in the dressing room and I suspect they came from that. Nothing there to worry your heads about, my dears," assures Bunty patronisingly.

"But did you see an epipen?" repeats Ben.

"No, there was no epipen. But I'm telling you, he didn't die from a bee sting. There would have been no need for an epipen."

"And you didn't touch the body at all?"

"No need to. He was obviously dead."

"Thank you. So the last time you saw him alive was that morning in the pharmacy when he bought travel sickness pills," says Grace.

"Yes, and now the mystery about that has been solved, hasn't it? Fancy him and Titania running off to Gretna! I didn't have an inkling about that. Well, none of us did. I was just talking to Mimi and …"

"Thank you, Mrs Beaufort," Grace cuts in. "We'll let you get back to the chemist shop. Although, I believe you only work part-time now?"

"That's right. I'm taking gradual retirement. I was finding that the responsibility of the pharmacy was getting too much for me so it's good to share the dispensing with someone else," she says.

"Oh yes, there was some… trouble, wasn't there? An old gentleman taking an overdose or something?" asks Grace slyly.

"It was nonsense," asserts Bunty defensively. "Fuss about nothing. I was completely exonerated by the coroner. Either he took too many tablets, or his weasel family gave him too many. They suggested I'd put the wrong dosage on the label, but no-one could find a bottle or packet afterwards so the coroner said that he could not believe that a pharmacist with my years of experience and a spotless reputation would have made such an elementary mistake. That family slunk away with their tails between their legs, I can tell you. You can ask anyone in the …"

"Thank you," interrupts Grace. "That will be all for now. Oh, and good luck with the panto, if it goes ahead."

"I can't see that it will. It would just be rude, wouldn't it? Poor old Bertram not even in his grave yet. Good sense must prevail," says Bunty staunchly as she gets up to leave.

Grace signals to me that they need more coffee so I busy myself with the kettle and the mugs, listening all the while and hoping they'll go back to the epipen. I don't have to wait long, as Ben is straight in with a question.

"How come there was an epipen by the body that our two experts didn't see?" he asks.

"Apparently it was underneath him. He must have fallen on top of it," explains Grace. Then she calls over to me for some of my home-made shortbread biscuits, and Ben's little face lights up. I like a lad with a good appetite.

"We'd better get Leela in before closing time," says Ben. "Shall I give her a call?"

While he's doing that, I take the tray over. I also tell Grace about the amber necklace and the rumours about Mimi accepting presents from her elderly clients. I hope I'm not being a sneak, but I think she needs to have all the information so she can make a judgement about Bertram's possible blackmail activities. Money makes the world go wrong.

Leela arrives, saying she's had a really busy morning with villagers phoning up about Bertram's death, ostensibly asking about funeral flowers but really wanting to know the gory details. Leela won't have been averse to telling them, either.

"Ah, Mrs Davies, do come around," calls Grace on hearing her voice. "We're just indulging in an afternoon cuppa, if you'd like to join us."

Leela cheekily takes her to mean that she can join them in coffee and biscuits so she orders a latte with an almond slice. Fortunately this seems to amuse Grace rather than annoy her. Leela seems to be glad that she's out of her shop for a while and is so relaxed that she starts chatting about the panto!

"I feel as if a weight has been lifted off my shoulders, dear," she enthuses. "Greaty has seen sense and the panto has been cancelled. Well, postponed. He's just phoned me. He thinks it will be just as fitting to have it in January. He says all the professional pantos go on well into the New Year, and the cast will have time to get used to him as an Ugly Sister. He'll probably completely re-cast the Horse. It doesn't require much acting ability, after all. Tony won't want to have someone different in front of him in such an intimate costume, and I can't imagine anyone else would want to be in Titty's place. I wouldn't trust him anywhere near my bum. A postponement is the least Greaty can do under the circumstances. I'm so relieved," she says, munching happily. "Now, what can I help you with?"

"We've just received a crucial piece of information, actually," Grace starts – and Leela is just about drooling to find out what that is. "Yes, it appears that Bertram was lying on top of an epipen."

Leela strikes the table in triumph. "I knew it! I knew it!" she asserts. "He was stung, wasn't he? It's all been a fuss about nothing. Oh, I don't mean 'nothing'. It's all very sad. But it was an accident, wasn't it? He didn't use his epi in time, did he?"

She's beaming as she licks her sticky fingers, thinking that an accidental death would be sad but acceptable.

"I wish that were the case, Mrs Davies, "but I'm afraid not. You see, it was the epipen that contained the poison."

Blimey! I almost drop the kettle. So that's how the poor bloke died. There's no doubt now about whether it was murder or not. I think I'd been hoping against hope that there would be an innocent explanation for his death. When Leela sounded so sure it was a bee sting just now, I started to believe it. I wish it had been. It's brought the fact of murder home to me and it's not a pleasant feeling. You think you know people, and then something happens out of the bloom that makes you look at everyone with suspicion.

Leela is just as floored as I am. No doubt she's thinking everything that I'm thinking.

"That's dreadful," she says. "So it is murder, and it must have been planned in advance. Premeditated."

"I'm afraid so. We have to go over everyone's movements with a fine toothcomb. For elimination purposes, can you just confirm when you last saw Bertram?"

"That's easy. It was eleven o'clock and he came in for a buttonhole, a yellow rose. I thought it was strange but he just smiled when I asked him what the celebration was. Quite intriguing at the time though we all know now about him and Titty, don't we?"

"Did you talk about anything else?" asks Ben.

"Not that I remember. Maybe the usual small talk about the weather. Maybe the rehearsal and the reporter that night. I can't remember anything particular so there can't have been anything significant."

"The work on your basement room, perhaps?" asks Ben, seemingly innocently.

"The job was done and dusted. There wasn't anything more to say," she replies decisively.

"No more money to be paid?" he continues.

"No. He'd been paid in full. It was a bit more expensive than I'd expected but it was a good job."

Grace follows up quietly with "Was it expensive because he had to remove asbestos? Or did he just cover it up?"

Leela freezes. All her bonhomie drains away in an instant. Maybe she's thinking it's a fair cop, maybe she's wondering if she can feign ignorance. Before she can say anything, Grace reveals that Wendy's 'aluminium' has been interpreted as asbestos. Leela sighs dramatically and nods.

"Bertram said there was asbestos down there and that a specialist firm would charge thousands to remove it. Covering it up - safely - would mean I could sell the shop and retire with a bit of profit. I stress that he said it was done safely. He was terrifying Wendy, too, saying that no-one would want to buy her fabrics if they thought they were covered in asbestos dust, so she would need to have the same sort of job done in her basement room. But, I'm wondering now if it wasn't all a big scam. I wouldn't put it past him to have invented the asbestos just to screw some money out of us. Bastard."

"I expect you're quite glad he's dead," says Ben.

"What are you implying, young man?" huffs Leela.

"Absolutely nothing, Mrs Davies. I was just …" he apologises.

"Just don't, then. I would never kill another human being, particularly not for such a flimsy reason. I can't even kill bees, and I'm at risk whenever I see one."

"You and Bertram, it seems. Do you carry an epipen?" asks Grace.

"Of course. Always. It's here in my bag now," and she takes it out to show them.

"All present and correct!" says Grace lightly. "Thank you. And thank you for being so honest about the blackmail."

"Extortion," mutters Ben.

"I wouldn't call it that," argues Leela. "I was just paying a little more for peace of mind and safety."

"Finally, what were your movements on the evening of the murder?"

"I closed the shop at six, went home to change and spruce myself up a bit for the possible photographs for the newspaper, and went straight on to the Hall, getting there at about five to seven. The rest you know."

My mind is working overtime on the blackmail theme. Would Leela resort to murder to make sure her sale went through? I can't see it myself but then how well do we really know our friends and neighbours? It's a sobering thought.

Grace and Ben decide that they need a breath of fresh air before concluding their interviews, so Ben phones asking Jack to come in, knowing that it will take him nearly half an hour to get here. A little walk round the village seems in order, and I must say I'm pleased to take a break as well.

Chapter 15

Knowing that it will take Jack a bit more than
twenty minutes to get from the site to the village,
Grace and Ben haven't got long for their refreshing
walk and Tom and I haven't got long to unwind
before the next onslaught of questioning. I must say
I'm knackered. I know I haven't been buzzing
round the café with customers' orders like Tom but
my mental agility has been sorely tried. I've made
up a time-line for everybody's sightings of Bertram
and for their movements all afternoon till the
rehearsal. Frankly, it's hard to see who could
possibly have killed Bertram between five and
seven. Tom says that the fact that the poison was
delivered by the epipen is mind-blowing. It really
is. How on earth can anyone have put poison into
Bertram's epi without his knowing it? He would
never let anyone touch it. And even if someone
somehow managed to put poison into it, why on
earth would Bertram inject himself when there were
no live bees around? It's winter, after all. Those
dead bees on the floor of the toilet were so
obviously dead, according to Bunty, that they
wouldn't have scared him. Instead of getting us
closer to a solution, I feel it's become more

complicated than ever. I can't see the wood for the bees.

Tom and I are just fortifying ourselves with coffee eclairs (much better than chocolate, in my opinion) when Greatorex breezes in.

"May I join you?" he asks suavely.

"Of course. Coffee and cake?" I say resignedly. No peace for the wicket.

"Excellent. I'll have what you're having. When in Rome…"

We squidge our way through the eclairs in our different styles: I bite into it greedily, letting the cream explode messily; Tom does the same but more gently, so the cream merely puffs out at the side; Greaty uses a pastry fork and takes tiny pieces without any mess at all. Don't you just hate people who can do that?

"I've decided to postpone the panto, Jenny," he says, and I act all surprised. "If the professionals can expand into January, I think we owe it to them to follow suit. Our audience might have felt awkward about cheering us on knowing that Bertram, like Elvis, had left the building."

Tom and I are nodding sagely. I must say I'm relieved, just like Leela. A panto is a bit of fun and needs the laughter and co-operation of the audience to work. Nobody would have felt like cheering and jeering, and the whole evening would have fallen as flat as a branflake.

"I'll step in as the second Ugly Sister, of course. I was wondering if you would like to tread the boards, too?" he asks sweetly.

"Not this time, Greaty. I'll happily carry on as Prompt but I really don't want to be either half a horse or anything else. I'll be very interested when you come to do 'The Cherry Orchard', though."

"What? Oh, I don't think that will ever be on the cards. Too depressing," he says dismissively. "But don't worry about the panto casting. I'm sure I shall easily replace the Croppers."

"Perhaps Tony will still be willing to be a horse's arse," says Tom cheekily, which makes even Greaty smile.

"I rather think that his proximity to the front's rear end - if you see what I mean – will dissuade many a young hopeful. No, it will be better to recast the whole horse. I don't anticipate any difficulties. Any nice young couple will do."

We've just finished scraping up the last of the cream (well, in my case, licking it off the plate) when Jack comes in. It's taken him twenty-five minutes and he's puffing like a grampus. He's surprised to see Greaty here and rushes to assure him that all's well at the site. Greaty sighs and says he'd better get back there before half the two-by-fours have been walked off to help to construct various workers' sheds and outhouses. Nice to know he has such faith in his workforce! He's just paying when a rosy-cheeked Grace and a rosy-nosed Ben arrive back from their constitutional.

"Ah, Mr Gofer," says Grace apologetically, "I hope we haven't kept you waiting? Do come into our little office area," she says, and I can't help adding 'said the spider to the fly' in my head.

We all resume our places, with me tucked into my Little Jack Horner. Poor old Tom is left to clear up again. You know, I think he'll be more appreciative from now on of the hard work I do on my feet all day here in the café.

"Sorry to have left you till last, Mr Gofer," says Ben. "I hope you haven't felt left out."

"Course not," says Jack bluffly. "To be honest, I wish I didn't 'ave to be 'ere at all."

"Indeed. We'd all rather be somewhere else but we have rather a nasty murder to clear up first. So can we just ascertain what your movements were yesterday afternoon?"

"Same as ever. When there's a job on, I'm at the site all the time. I was there all day."

"Can anyone confirm that?" asks Ben.

"Well I wasn't working on my own, was I? I was either in the site office with Greaty or supervising the men. Goody popped over at about four just to remind me about the reporter being there before the rehearsal. Good old sis, I think she was worried that seeing little Jane Makepeace might be a shock – you know, after the unpleasantness last time."

"Remind me," says Grace. "What was that all about?"

"Little Jane is a henvironmentalist, with emphasis on the mental. Some nasty chemicals were dumped during the time when Greatorex was constructing 'is last development, and just because the site was an old chemical plant, she jumped to the conclusion that the chemicals must 'ave come from the site. She got the Environment Inspectors in an' all. Obviously, no connection was found, but she made our lives bloody difficult. It was a slur on our reputations, and builders depend on the good reports of their clients. Me and Greaty, we were being tarred with a nasty brush. It sent me spiralling down and it took a while to get through it. Greaty 'ad to drop the price of the 'ouses, and I was short of work for a few months. It all got back to normal as soon as the Inspectors left and we were proved innocent, but it took me a time to get back on an even keel."

"Were you proved innocent, or was it a case of the Scottish 'not proven'?" asks Grace.

"Now look 'ere, I'm not going through all that again. There was no evidence against us – because we didn't do nothing wrong!" splutters Jack.

It's on the tip of my tongue to point out that his double negative says the very opposite of what he means to say, but I hold back. I'm not supposed to be listening, after all.

"Let's move on, shall we? Did you see Bertram that afternoon?" asks Ben, getting us back to the present.

"Yeah. He was at the site in the early p.m.. Greaty saw 'im and then 'e came over to chat to me. Must 'ave been about two or two thirty."

"You've heard that he was eloping with Titania that very afternoon, have you?"

"I 'ave now. I didn't know then."

"Why do you think he walked all the way over to the building site on the very afternoon that he was running off with Titania?" asks Grace.

"I'm blowed if I know. He just stood and chatted for a while. Maybe 'e was killing time till 'is train was due. Search me," says Jack.

"Was that the last time you saw him?"

"No, you know it wasn't. I've already told you that I saw him in the pub car park at five."

"For another little chat?" asks Ben innocently.

"Look, there's nothing suspicious about seeing a mate and 'aving a chat. I'd hardly ignore 'im, would I?" says Jack, and I can see he's getting a bit angry about Ben's question.

"I was just wondering if Bertram had asked you for some money up at the site earlier, and you'd told him to meet you in the car park later to collect it?" says Ben.

"What? What's this about? Why would I be giving 'im money?"

"Exactly," says Grace. "Why would you?"

"This is rubbish," blusters Jack. "I didn't owe 'im any money. He just passed the time of day, that's all. Then he drove off towards the Village 'all – which is also towards the station."

"If he was going to the station, why did he end up in the Hall?" pursues Grace.

"Am I a bleeding clairvoyant? How should I know? Maybe 'e needed a pee before getting on the train. Them train loos can be pretty disgusting."

I'm feeling pretty sorry for Jack now. They're really grilling him.

"And I'll 'ave you know that I couldn't of done 'im in, anyway. I went straight into the pub for a pie and chips before the rehearsal and the bar staff can vouch for me that I didn't leave there till it was time to go up to the theatre at ten to seven. Ask them. They'll tell you."

Jack looks mighty relieved to be able to give them his cast-iron alibi and Grace is nodding and smiling as if butter wouldn't meld. It's as if she wanted to see just how upset he could get. When she tells him he can go, he's sweating like a fig. I'm remembering how much that questioning by the Environmental Inspectors affected him. Goody had thought he was heading for a nervous breakdown.

She's always worried about him, ever since he was a tearaway kid getting into trouble all the time. He had a little spell At Her Majesty's Pleasure for stealing a car and joy-riding it into a very solid tree. Where Goody took elocution lessons and got herself onto the education ladder, poor old Jack stayed working class and proud of it. She had to give him a lot of support but he had seemed to turn the corner and settle down. I could understand her worry that the suspicion about the chemical dumping might send him in into a depression. She's a good Big Sis.

I take a glass of water over to Grace and Ben. They must have been parched after their walk and they'd had no chance to drink anything with Jack being questioned straight away. That makes me sound so concerned for their welfare, doesn't it? Well, I am – but I also want to hear what their latest ideas are.

"Oh, thanks, Jenny. Why don't you take a seat? We need your statement as well so we might as well get it now. Where were you yesterday afternoon?"

I can't help laughing. I tell them that I was here in the café all day long until six o'clock when Tom and I closed up together and went home for a swift bite to eat before the rehearsal. Where on earth does she think I'd be?

"And did you see Bertram at all?" asks Ben.

"He usually comes in for a sausage roll or something at lunch time, except on his days off," I reply. "And it was his day off, so he didn't grace us with his presence. I didn't see him at all. It was a busy day, as usual, and I didn't even spot him passing by. Sorry."

"I thought that would be the case, judging by today, but I needed to ask," says Grace apologetically. "Actually, you've been a great help to us and I wonder if you'd mind my plumbing your knowledge of the area a bit?"

"Plumb away," I say.

"I'm aware that you've been able to hear some of the interviews…"

I thought to myself that I'd heard the lot if she did but know it, but I don't say anything.

"…and I'm sure you have picked up that the poison was administered via Bertram's own epipen. I wondered if you had any ideas about how someone around here could get hold of any noxious substance?"

"There's obviously the chemist's but you'd have to have a prescription," I muse.

"Or be the actual pharmacist," interposes Ben.

"Then there's the District Nurse's supplies," I continue.

"Which would be accessible not only to the District Nurse herself but also to anyone who could get into her bag," interrupts Ben again.

"Anyone could have rat poison, of course. All the villagers have had trouble with mice and rats at some point – it's par for the gorse in the countryside," I add. "There was also that chemical spill a little while ago. Whoever dumped it could have kept some. Or whoever helped clear it up."

"That's what I was afraid of," sighs Grace. "Almost anyone could have got hold of poison if they really wanted to. Our analysts at the lab will have to pinpoint it more specifically before we can be sure. I'm expecting their call very soon. Well, thanks, Jenny. You and Tom have been stars today. If we'd had to use the station at Wellesley Ayrton this would have taken so much longer and been a total disruption for everyone."

"You're welcome. Any idea if you'll need the space tomorrow?" I ask, half hoping they will so I can keep up with developments, and half hoping they won't so we can have a rest!

"I'll let you know. Ben and I have some good ideas and we need to pull it all together. The notebook you found has been invaluable, I must say. We may even be ready to make an arrest tonight…"

Wow! My gasted has never so flabbered. Tom and I will have to put our heads together and see what we can figure out. I must admit I can't see my way through the fog right now. It's a real pea-snooper. Nearly everyone seems to have a possible motive, but also a possible alibi. There will be much pondering in the Brandon kitchen tonight!

"While we were having our little break just now, Ben and I drove up to the Village Hall to have another look around," says Grace. "There was a notice on the door of the hall saying that today's Toddler crèche was cancelled because the toilets were out of bounds. Very sensible. You can't expect little ones not to use the loo, and children's safety must be absolutely paramount. Can you believe it, we found a drawing pin attached to some sticky tape in the corridor, too, so some little kid might have had an accident if they'd fallen on that. People are very thoughtless sometimes. No-one was around and Bertram's car was the only one in the car park. It was securely locked but we could see that there was a suitcase in the boot. Our colleagues had searched the car park and the surrounding area very thoroughly and they reported nothing unusual. The bushes revealed nothing more sinister than a shopping trolley and enough sweet wrappers to fill a bin bag. So our only clues as to the murderer are in people's statements. As I said, we have some ideas..."

She obviously isn't going to share them with me, more's the pity. She and Ben prepare to be on their way, promising to let us know in good time if they want the café tomorrow. Still, I think Tom and I know just as much as she does, so we'll pull our ideas together tonight and see where it leads us. When Grace and Ben leave, we take an executive decision to close early. We fill up the dishwasher (oh yes, all mod cons in my café) and do a quick tidy and sweep before heading home.

Chapter 16

When we get home, the first thing we do is pour ourselves a very large G & T and collapse onto the sofa. The sun is nowhere near the yard-arm here in Middle Pidding, but it must be there in some far-flung corner of the globe!

"My feet are throbbing," complains Tom plaintively. "They could join the rhythm section of a rock band and earn us a bit of pocket money."

"Poor lambkin," I commiserate. I'm on the point of saying that that's how I feel at the end of every day but I hold back. It's better if he comes to realise that by himself. Discretion is the better part of velour. The G & T doesn't touch the sides and we're soon heading to the kitchen for a refill. We both love cooking, but there are times when a take-away is an absolute necessity, and this is one of them. I hunt through the odds-and-sods drawer for the local Indian menu which is two years out of date so the prices won't be right, but we don't care as long as they still serve up the same dishes. While we wait for it to arrive, I quickly make some raita and Tom steams some rice – we resent paying for things that we can knock up ourselves in two shakes of a lamb's nail. It must be a slow night for the restaurant, because the meal arrives in twenty minutes and we're soon sitting down and stuffing ourselves with excellent Indian cuisine. We hold back from discussing the case until we've satisfied the rumble-tums.

"Who's your Prime Suspect?" I ask Tom.

"I'm flummoxed," he replies. "Honest to god, it could be any one of them."

"On the other hand, it can't be any of them either!" I joke, but it's no joke really. "Lots of them have got motives and all of them have got alibis."

"The only ones we can definitely rule out are Chris and Freddy because of the train hold-up. They were well out of the way. I can't see that they have a reason to kill Bertram, either."

"Well, the notebook has a C, which could be Chris, with an X after it," I say.

"But with a question mark, so it sounds like it was just a possibility for the future. I can't think what he could have on Chris, mind you."

"Mmmm. I think he might be gay. He got so het up about little Jane just turning up on his doorstep and taking a photo of his 'guest', whoever that was," I muse.

"People don't get blackmailed for being gay nowadays, love," scoffed Tom.

"They might if they haven't come out. He might not want his work to know, or his family."

"Maybe. But it's not a motive for murder, is it?"

"No, you're right. And his alibi is water-tight anyway, so let's dismiss him – and Freddy – from the list."

"That leaves everybody else!"

"Except us. Grace and Ben have got their work cut out for them. I'm glad we don't do this for a living."

Our mobile phones both ping at the same time. We simultaneously reach for our own and realise as soon as we look at them that they have come from Grace and so will be identical. Here's what they say:

> The Village Hall has been closed by order of the Council and the police. Therefore we shall be using it as our investigation centre from now on.

I am calling everyone to the Hall at 10 a.m. tomorrow. I realise that this will disrupt your working day but a murder investigation is of primary importance and I must insist that you all attend.

Please be aware that the Toilets will be closed off and therefore unable to be used.

D.I. Grace Jones

"Hellfire!" erupts Tom. "What are we supposed to do? Cross our legs? Stock up with Tena Lady? Doesn't she realise that those of us who are middle-aged need to frequent the loo more frequently?"

I can't help giggling. Tom is a bit of a slave to his prostate, which isn't really funny, I know, but his unnecessary embarrassment about it just makes me laugh. He's more worried about that than losing the profit from a closed café.

"I'll take a milk bottle along so you can have a secret pee in the corner!"

"Not funny, Jen. It means I can't have my usual mugs of tea at breakfast. Why on earth does she want us to be there all together at ten? Is she going to interview us one at a time in the kitchen while the rest of us stew in the hall? It's ridiculous."

"Maybe she wants to do a Miss Marble on us. You know, the Startling Dénouement," I suggest, stroking his back to calm him down.

"Well, I hope it doesn't take too much time or there won't be a dry seat in the house!"

"Do you feel like doing some baking for the café?" I ask, thinking it might take his mind off his bladder.

"I suppose we'd better, although we'll be losing our morning trade so we won't need to do much," Tom says, and I'm glad he's getting back to normal and thinking of shekels.

"What do you say to opening the café at 8.30 as usual for breakfasts? I bet all the cast would come in, and lots of our regulars on their way to work," I suggest.

"Not to mention the nosey parkers who'll want to know what's going on in the investigation. It's not every day we have a murder to solve in the village," agrees Tom, brightening considerably. "Come on. We'll need scones and bacon rolls for the breakfast crowd, then sausage rolls and coleslaw for lunch, then chocolate cake for tea time."

"Assuming we'll be back in the café for lunch…" I venture.

"Of course we will. Startling Dénouements never last for more than a morning!"

We set to with a will. I'm glad to see the enthusiasm return to Tom's demeanour. That's one of the things I love about him, his energy and vigour. After a day in the café, I often think I would just collapse on the sofa if it wasn't for Tom herding me into the kitchen. He's my lifeline and I can't imagine life without him. We're soul mutes. This gets me wondering about Titania.

"Poor old Titty. I wonder if she's been escorted back to Pidding by now."

"At least she can't be a suspect," says Tom.

"No, but I bet this is the last place she wants to be. I mean, she can't go home to Tony and she'll want to avoid being anywhere near him, won't she?"

"Where will she go?"

"Oh, that was one of the things I picked up today. Goody said she could stay with her."

"I expect the police will make sure she's safe from Tony's anger. I've come to realise what a nasty piece of work he is. I sometimes wondered about the bruises she had on her arms at times, but she used to say that she was just one of those people who bruised easily. Now I think there might have been hidden injuries that she was afraid to talk about," says Tom.

"The only person she talked to was Goody. I'm glad she had one staunch friend to rely on. Although Goody would have preferred it if Titty stayed here…"

"…but only if she was safe. It was very selfless of Goody to help her escape the clutches of a controlling husband even though it meant that she'd lose her mate."

We are surprised by a knock on the door. Why does that always happen at the most inconvenient times, when you're up to your elbows in suds or extricating your sticky fingers from dough? I'm the easiest to clean off, so I run to the front door. It's a policeman, but not young Ben. My heart skips a beat – I don't know why as I've got nothing to fear, but it's just a natural reaction to seeing the police on your doorstep. I stand there with my mouth open, goldfish-like, unable to decide if I need to ask him in or not. He's quick to reassure me.

"Sorry to bother you, madam. May we have a quick search of your garage?" he says politely.

"Garage?" I repeat, as if he was speaking a foreign language. "Yes, I suppose so. What are you looking for?"

"Just routine, madam. Is it open?" he replies, not answering my question.

"It's always open, dear. I expect you'll find that every garage in our village is left open."

"Ah," he smiles, "a good old-fashioned trusting community."

Off he trots to the side of the house. Tom comes up behind me and we both stand watching the young copper disappear into our garage.

"I suppose I should accompany him," says Tom uncertainly.

"It wouldn't hurt. Just in case he's planting a stash of heroin or something," I joke. "See if you can find out if it's just us or a more general search."

Tom goes into the garage through the door from the kitchen so he doesn't have to change out of his slippers. I can hear them talking but I can't make out what they're saying, which makes me impatient for his return. It doesn't take long.

"Well?" I ask.

Tom laughs at my eagerness and comes to the sink to wash his hands.

"I've been like Patience on a vol-au-vent," I say, which makes him smile.

"He asked if we had any pesticide or rat poison. I told him we hadn't but he insisted on looking for himself. There's a team going round all the villagers, apparently, but I bet they're concentrating on our little panto party."

"They're trying to trace poisons, aren't they? Their problem will be that lots of people have vermin poisons tucked away at the back of their garages. It's a rural village, for goodness sake."

"Their labs will have narrowed it down by now," he says confidently..

For a moment I have this picture in my head of a team of Labradors sniffing out the culprit poison. When I tell this to Tom, he insists on cuddling me even though his hands are still soaking wet! We hurry on with our preparations for the next day and with our usual teamwork we whizz through it.

Bedtime can't come quickly enough. I'm absolutely knickered.

Chapter 17

Neither of us slept well, tossing and turning with excitement even though we were exhausted. We'd sent a Reply All to Grace's memo telling everyone that we'd be open for brekky, and we get in to the café at eight o'clock so that we can take down the screen and the curtains. It is so nice to have my little goldmine back to normal. As our lovely cast arrives, they help us set out the tables and chairs in the usual pattern and I can put on my two kettles to get coffee on the go. I knew everyone would come here to exchange news and views before going up to the Hall. A cast is like a little family and a disaster brings out the best in us. Although I suppose it didn't bring out the best in one of us, as far as Bertram was concerned.

Jack opens the discussion with "Did anyone else's garage get searched last night?"

It appears that everyone's did. I think we all feel a bit better, knowing that we weren't singled out. Jack certainly looks relieved.

"What on earth were they looking for?" asks Wendy, and we all look at her in disbelief that she hasn't worked it out for herself.

"Poison, dear," replies Mimi kindly. "They actually asked me if I kept any in the garage and then they asked me to check my supplies of medicines to see if anything was missing. It wasn't, by the way. They're obviously trying to find the source of the poison in Bertram's epipen."

So the news has spread about the epipen. Trust the village grapevine.

"Well I think it's a damn cheek," says Greaty. "The only person who could have tampered with Bertram's epipen was Bertram himself. Can you imagine him letting someone else handle it, even momentarily? He was paranoid about keeping himself safe. The only solution is that he <u>did</u> commit suicide, no matter how difficult we find that to believe."

"Not when he was about to elope. That doesn't make sense," asserts Leela.

"Maybe he was regretting that. Maybe he couldn't face the prospect of marriage to Titty. She isn't all hearts and flowers. I should know!" says Tony venomously.

There's a slightly embarrassed silence after that because we're all thinking that a man who's generous with his fists doesn't make a pleasant person to be with. Frankly, our sympathy lies with Titty. Goody gives him a cold stare.

"Where is Titty?" asks Bunty.

"She stayed with me last night," explains Goody, sending a challenging look to Tony. "The police reclaimed her this morning for more questioning. She was so upset, poor girl."

Tony sneers, but the rest of us are feeling truly sorry for her. What a way for her dreams to be shattered. She must be absolutely down in the mumps. We're all needing a bit of a boost, so it's a good job I made extra croissants. I feel rather like the Good Samaritan binding up people's wounds and giving them some comfort. Food is one of life's richest blessings, I always think.

Breakfast is just about over when Grace and Ben surprise us with their presence. It isn't ten o'clock yet but somehow we all feel guilty for sitting around chomping. They say a pleasant 'Good morning' before ordering take-away coffees and heading up to the Hall, saying we can join them when we're ready. As they stare at all the crumb-laden plates, we feel very conscious of our selfish hedonism. Everyone hurries to pay and they're falling over themselves to leave the café and get up to the meeting. Tom and I look at each other, debating whether to clear up first or just high-tail it to follow them. We don't want to miss anything, that's the truth of it, so we just leave the mess and follow on, leaving an apologetic notice on the door promising to be open for lunch.

Grace and Ben sit us in a circle and we look around at each other expectantly, even excitedly. For one of us there must be a sense of foreboding, I suppose, but nothing is showing on the outside. Looking at each face in turn, I can't catch anything resembling guilt or worry. Someone is giving the performance of their life.

"I shall wind this up as quickly as I can," says Grace cheerily, as if this was the Women's Institute AGM instead of a murder enquiry. I expect she wants to put the innocent at ease while scaring the bejesus out of the culprit. "First of all, we know that Bertram was a blackmailer."

"Extortionist," whispers Ben.

"And that he was … extorting money from a lot of people here in this room."

That puts the cat among the widgets. Eyes are swivelling, hands are fidgeting, throats are cleared. No-one actually says anything but looks speak volumes. It seems as if Grace is waiting for people to object, and when they don't, she smiles smugly.

"A very useful notebook of Bertram's was found in which he wrote down his victims and how much they paid him."

That causes a couple of gasps and downward glances.

"Unfortunately it was in code but it was such a simple one that it was easy to penetrate. Who shall we start with? How about you, Mr Manston?"

Greaty flares his nostrils alarmingly and starts to bluster, but Grace cuts through his huffing.

"Bertram wrote GD in his book, the G standing for Greatorex and the D denoting the Roman 500. A whacking great £500, Mr Manston. Now what could you possibly have done which was worth £500 to cover up?"

"This is ridiculous!" explodes Greaty. "A 'G' could point to a great many people. The village must have tens of people whose names start with G. There's Goody for a start."

Poor Goody looks appalled that he could point the finger at her. She would never have done the same to him. Perhaps this will open her eyes and convince her that he just isn't worth the effort.

"Come now, Mr Manston. You are undoubtedly the richest person in the room, and probably in the whole village. Blackmailers are clever estimators of the wealth of their victims and would never have expected someone like Goody to be able to pay out such a large sum."

"And 'er proper name isn't Goody, either," says Jack defensively, and it's nice to see him sticking up for his big sis instead of the other way round. "It was a nickname from school. Goody Two-Shoes. Violet is 'er real name."

"The question is: what did Bertram have on you, Mr Manston?" persists Grace.

"Could it be connected to that infamous chemical spill?" asks Ben, seemingly innocently. "Had Bertram dug up something – perhaps literally?"

"I'm thoroughly fed up with this slur on my reputation. I shall be contacting my solicitor!" fumes Greaty.

"Then there's JX," says Grace, moving on smoothly and ignoring Greaty's bluster. "J for Jack. So, Jack, it seems you could only be relied on for £10 at a go, although you coughed it up three times. What was your little secret?"

"Wait a minute, 'ang on there. I've got nothing to cover up."

"Except perhaps that you literally covered up a chemical dump for the man who gave you most of your work. You wouldn't want to upset Mr Manston by refusing, would you?" insinuates Ben.

"I was exonerated by the Investigators. We both were," splutters Jack. "Nothing was found. Nothing connected us to the poisoned stream."

"Did Bertram see you fly-tipping? Perhaps he took some incriminating photographs?"

"There's no proof. Nothing was found. 'ow dare you?" growls Jack. There's panic in his eyes and I can see Goody looking at him worriedly.

Grace carries on: "Obviously you cleared everything away before the Inspectors arrived, but you must have had quite a scare. No doubt you and Greatorex eradicated any mess, but Bertram still had some sort of proof, didn't he? A search of his room last night proved very interesting. A nice little cache of photos was discovered under a loose floorboard."

A deflated Jack sinks onto his chair and stares hopelessly at Greaty. Jane Makepeace looks like a plump little carp, her mouth open and her eyes wide. She gasps, "I knew it. I was right. My article focused on you two and I nearly got the sack for it."

"Your bloody article started the whole fiasco!" explodes Jack. "If it hadn't been for you, Bertram would never 'ave ..."

"Shut up, Jack," Greaty thunders.

Grace smilingly says, "But was all that enough to push either of you into murder? You would have lost a lot of money, either from being exposed or by continuing to pay Bertram to keep quiet, but would that lead you to murder? Let's leave that in abeyance for now. Does anyone else have reason to want Bertram out of the way? Let's look at the other possible victims of his blackmail."

"Extortion," whispers Ben.

"What on earth did he have on two such lovely ladies as Wendy and Leela?" continues Grace, turning suddenly to face them.

Greaty and Jack look relieved to have the attention taken away from them, and Goody pats her brother's arm gently. Everyone else just gasps at the thought of Wendy and Leela doing anything worthy of blackmail. Sorry, extortion.

"Asbestos!" says Grace. "Bertram covered it up for you, Leela, didn't he, so that you could sell your shop? No sale, no retirement, no round-the-world cruise. What a blow that would have been. And he was going to do the same for your little basement room, wasn't he, Wendy? Your precious fabrics needed to be protected. People wouldn't want to buy contaminated goods, would they? His silence would have saved you both a lot of money, so he obviously thought he deserved a share of it."

Wendy and Leela bow their heads in shame as their skulduggery is revealed. Neither of them is denying it, I notice.

"Is that enough to murder for?" asks Grace, staring at their flushed faces. "Or is that just a red herring?"

"She said fishily," quips Robbie.

"Which brings us to you, Mr Slack."

Robbie obviously wishes he'd kept his mouth shut as Grace's penetrating gaze falls on him.

"Fiddling the pub's books, were you? You said you'd found Bertram looking through your accounts. You tried to make it seem that you were concerned that he was swindling you but it was the other way round, wasn't it? You were the swindler and Bertram had enough evidence to show the brewery. We found a draft letter in with the photos welching on you. If he'd sent it, you and your wife would have been out of a job and facing a charge."

"It was circumstantial. There might have been the occasional slip of the pen but that sort of thing happens to everyone. I could have convinced the brewery that I was innocent. Years of faithful service would have saved me," asserts Robbie.

"But it was easier to drop him the odd ten quid, wasn't it?" says Ben.

"Look," says Robbie. "I didn't like the bloke, but I'd hardly have murdered him over it, would I? Be reasonable."

"What? Your reputation besmirched? No brewery wanting to employ you again? How would you and your wife have managed? It seems like a fairly substantial motive to me," says Grace. "And talking of reputations, what about you, Mimi? The respectable and trusted District Nurse. What did he have on you that was worth £50 a pop?"

"For goodness sake, what am I supposed to have done?" asks Mimi, throwing her hands up in the air and appealing to everyone round the room.

"Just a little matter of putting pressure on your patients. A nice bracelet here, a pretty necklace there, a mention in a will everywhere..." says Ben airily.

"Rubbish. My families trust me absolutely. I stand by the Hippocratic oath."

"Hypocritic," mutters Robbie.

"They trust you, do they? Bertram had a little list. Names, phone numbers – all your patients past and present, with asterisks by some of them. Perhaps suspicious families had been moaning to their odd-job man while he fixed their intruder alarms. I think Bertram could have made quite a case for 'de-frocking' you (or whatever the word is for stripping a District Nurse of her regalia.) I'm not at all sure there couldn't have been serious criminal charges involved."

"Rubbish," says Mimi again, but she's a bit quieter this time.

"Talking of trust, Bunty, I think this is where you come in. We were puzzled at first that there was no

'B' on Bertram's list, until we were informed that your proper name was Elizabeth – and lo and behold, there was an 'E'! Looking through Bertram's secret cache, we found a pack of tablets issued by your pharmacy with the name of an old gentleman who had died on it. Had you printed the wrong dosage on there?"

Bunty nearly faints. Her hand goes to her heart and her face is as white as a sheep. I'm worrying if she's going to have a heart attack. We sometimes forget that she's retirement age because she looks so strong, but a weak heart wouldn't surprise me. Grace is obviously thinking on the same lines because she rushes to tell her that the label on the tablets was perfectly legitimate. The relief on Bunty's face is wonderful.

"No doubt Bertram led you to believe that the label was incriminating so that you'd pay up to keep him quiet. He was a nasty piece of work, this Bertram," explains Grace. "Even without proof, he'd started a whispering campaign against you which must have been very upsetting. You were desperate to retain the trust of the local people in your pharmacy. You must have wanted Bertram out of your life. Enough to kill him?"

"Of course not," says Bunty staunchly. "None of these so-called motives would have led anyone to murder. It's ridiculous."

Murmurs of assent ripple round the room. Huffs have never been huffier, sniffs have never been sniffier.

"Ah, but one of you did it," says Ben. "One of you is a murderer."

That shuts everyone up straight away.

"On we go," breezes Grace. "Of course, it may be that the killing had nothing to do with Bertram's nice little earner. They do say that most murders are committed by a member of the family, more specifically the spouse."

Tony rears up, rather like the horse he should have been playing. He opens his mouth to object but Ben is too quick for him.

"Knowing your wife was having an affair must have been like swallowing acid every day," says Ben.

"But I didn't know!" shouts Tony. "None of us knew. Except Miss Goody Two Shoes. Thanks so much for that, Goody!"

"We only have your word for that," says Grace. "Perhaps you'd been hoping that the affair would fizzle out and Titania would stay with you. When you found out about the Gretna Green plans, you had to do something more drastic."

"I tell you, I didn't know. If I'd found out, I'd have killed her, not him. I'm the one who's been wronged here. I'm the victim!"

"Well, I'd suggest that Bertram had a worse deal than you. However, it does bring us to the next issue. It seems obvious that this murder was planned well in advance. Somehow, poison had to be introduced to Bertram's epipen, leaving us with the riddle of how the poison was obtained and, even more puzzling, how was Bertram persuaded to let his epipen out of his sight?" continues Grace.

I must say, that's what has intrigued me and Tom. We can't think of an answer and, looking round the room, I don't think anyone else can either.

"You'll all be interested to know that rat poison was not the source, so those of you who had vermin exterminators in your sheds or garages can rest easier – though I would impress upon you all the need for caution in the storage of such contaminants."

I immediately look at Bunty and Mimi as being the only ones who could legitimately have access to real poisons. Everyone else is having the same thought, it seems, as all eyes are turned to them. They're both shaking their heads and looking panic-stricken.

"Do any of you have an epipen?" asks Grace, full knowing the answer.

"I do," says Leela, and her voice seems to have gone up an octave. "I'm allergic to bee stings. You all know that, it's no secret."

"Indeed. Anyone else?"

We're all shaking our heads, thanking heaven that we haven't got one of those wretched allergies. My cousin Florence is allergic to peanuts and it's a complete nightmare. She has to check the contents of everything she buys just in case. Every time she goes to a restaurant or to anyone's house for a meal, she has to make it clear that anything which has even been in the presence of a peanut is a source of danger. We just take our health for granted, don't we? Grace is staring at poor old Bunty again.

"If you're thinking that I could have stolen one from the pharmacy, let me tell you that every item in my shop is accounted for. There is no way I could have taken one. My records are immaculate and you can check them as minutely as you like," asserts Bunty.

"That goes for me, too," says Mimi.

"So, no other epipens around?" asks Grace.

Silence ensues. I happen to look up at Tom and I can see he's frowning. What has occurred to him, I'm wondering. What have I missed? After a minute or two, Greaty clears his throat and hesitantly reminds us that there is always one in the First Aid box at the side of the stage.

"Oh, of course," says Goody, jumping up as if she's had an electric shock. "Of course. I completely forgot about that."

She's up and running to the Stage Management corner. In fact, I've never seen her move so fast. She grabs the box and runs straight back to the circle of chairs.

"I can check if it's there, can't I?" she says breathlessly.

We're all on tenterhoops. Goody delves in the box and comes up triumphantly with the emergency epi. "Here it is. Thank goodness. This can't be the murder weapon," says Goody. "I would have felt terrible if someone had stolen this one and murdered Bertram with it."

"Now that is very interesting," muses Grace.

"It's obviously what I said to begin with," says Greaty rather haughtily. "The only explanation is that he killed himself. No-one had access to poison and no-one could have got to his epipen. Now can we all go home? We have businesses to run, you know."

"Not so fast, Mr Manston. Indulge me for just a little while longer. Let's just assume that this was not suicide, shall we? We've seen that there are many possible motives among you, some perhaps more plausible than others – though, as to that, what may seem trivial to most of us can be absolutely crucial in the mind of a murderer. But let's move on to the planning that must have gone into the fatal deed."

Greaty sits back down again reluctantly. I have to admit that I'm torn: part of me wants to get out of here quickly and get on with life in the café; part of me is dying to know whodunit and why. The fact that everyone else is sitting down and glancing round the circle makes me feel pretty sure that we all want to know where Grace and Ben are going with this.

"I think," says Grace, looking more and more like Miss Marble, "that everything revolves around bees. Bertram is allergic, and everyone knows it. What's more, he is terrified of the wee things, and everyone knows that too. At first, we assumed that the dead bees on the floor indicated live bees somewhere in the room. But we soon saw that the dead bees were practically antique, just husks that wouldn't have frightened anyone. Seeing them on the floor, even a hypochondriac like Bertram would simply have walked away, and certainly wouldn't have assumed that he needed to get out his epipen and inject himself. Could someone have introduced a live bee into the room, which would have caused such a panic?"

"It's bloody December! No bees, not even for ready money!" scoffs Jack, and we all smile.

"Exactly, Mr Gofer. It is, as you say, bloody December. Could someone have nurtured a few bees through the summer and trained them to home in on Bertram?"

Now we're all starting to giggle a bit. Trained bees! It's the picture of one of us in a top hat and tail-coat poised with whip in hand training a squad of bees. Jack flips his wrist as if he's cracking a whip and says, "Sit! Roll over! Attack!" Even Ben is smiling.

"No. Of course not," agrees Grace. "Then I remembered that Miss Makepeace had mentioned scratching her hand on the doorknob. Now, if that had happened to Bertram on going into the toilet and the next thing he saw was a dead bee, might he have had a moment of panic? So I went back and examined the doorknob..."

We're waiting with bated breath. You could cut the atmosphere with a knight.

"...but the doorknob was as smooth as a baby's bum," continues Grace. "However, I did find a drawing pin stuck to some sticky tape in the corridor. What if that had originally been stuck to the handle so that it felt like a sting to Bertram when he opened the door? Imagine you're Bertram. You touch the doorknob, you feel a piercing pain, you look down and see bees, you conclude that you've been stung, you panic, you go for your epipen and inadvertently inject yourself with the poison that kills you."

Believe me, we're all imagining it. That's the trouble with having a vivid imagination: you can picture things so clearly. Little Jane is looking down at the plaster on her palm, her mouth shaped like an O.

"That's really clever," says Jane.

"Cunning, certainly," agrees Grace. "And obviously planned carefully."

Tom's mulling it over. I recognise the little frown he has when he's wrestling with a Sudoku. Something's not adding up for him. Wait for it …here he goes:

"But, Grace, that still doesn't address the problem of how poison got into Bertram's epipen in the first place."

He's right. Greaty nods his head sagely and everyone looks with respect at my Tom and his logical brain, then back at Grace for the next piece of the jigsaw.

Grace is smiling and nodding her head, too. "That puzzled me for quite some time, Tom. The thing is, we're all assuming that Bertram would have used his own epipen if he'd felt a bee sting, and that therefore the poison would have been in his epi. But what if he used someone else's?"

Leela fairly screams, "No, no! He'd never have used someone else's when he'd got his own right there in his pocket. No-one would do that," she asserts – and surely she should know.

"Perhaps the murderer was right there, in the toilet, with poisoned epipen at the ready. It would have to be someone he trusted, of course. It would flash through his mind that an epipen in the hand was worth two in the bush, so to speak. No faffing around getting it out of his pocket, wasting time while the venom was taking hold. Here's a friend with one at the ready, saving his life."

"But actually taking his life," adds Ben seriously. "So Bertram's epipen remained pristine and unused. No tampering was necessary. After the fatal poisoning, our killer simply removed Bertram's unused epi and replaced it with the murderous one so that it would look as though poor old Bertram had injected himself with venom. So who had access to another epipen that they could tamper with at their leisure?"

All eyes swivel to Leela, who looks round with horror. "Not me. I didn't do it, I swear. You can't possibly think it was me."

To be honest, I can't see Leela as a killer, I really can't. Besides, hasn't she got an alibi? That obviously occurs to her as well, as she almost yelps in triumph.

"By the time I'd closed the shop, gone home and changed, eaten something with my husband, I couldn't possibly have been able to go to the theatre and fit all that in. My alibi is rock solid."

"So is mine!" ricochets round the room as everybody asserts that their alibis are foolproof. It's like "I am Spartacus" around here. Grace is still smiling. I don't know how she does it, ploughing on against all the odds. She hasn't finished tantalising us yet.

"On the face of it, you're all quite right that your alibis seem foolproof. But one of you was able to fit it all in. And I'm just about to tell you who."

You could hear a tin drop!

Chapter 18

Grace looks slowly at each one of us in turn. It's a withering look, I can tell you, full of interrogation and suspicion. She looks at me, and I immediately feel guilty, even though I'm as innocent as the day is long. I expect everyone is feeling the same under the searchlight of her gaze.

"That's how you did it, Goody. Isn't that right?" accuses Grace coolly.

A white-faced Goody gasps and shakes her head. "That's utter rubbish. For a start, I don't have an epipen so how could I possibly have doctored one?"

"But as the Stage Manager, you had access to one, didn't you? You were very eager to show me that the one in the First Aid box was still there untouched."

"Where do you suggest I got the poison from then? There was no rat poison in my garage ..." starts Goody.

"...and rat poison wasn't used anyway," adds Jack illogically.

"I'm suggesting, Miss Gofer, that you took some of the chemical waste that had been dumped by your brother on Mr Manston's orders."

All hell breaks loose! Jack's standing up and waving his fist at Grace, Ben steps in front of her to protect her, Goody holds her brother back, Greaty explodes into vehement denials and threats to call his lawyer, and the rest of us are shouting out either in anger at the accusations or in attempts to calm everyone down. It's a bear garden.

Ben's stentorian tones ring out: "Sit down and shut up!" It's not the language you expect from His Madge's constabulary but it does the trick.

Grace continues: "You've always tried to protect your younger brother, haven't you, just like a big sister should. I expect that you've dug him out of many a hole over the years. But he really seemed to have settled down, didn't he? Until the time he was working on the development on the old chemical plant and he came to confess to you what Mr Manston had told him to do. Did you help him to hide it by shoving it into the stream, not realising that that made its spread more traceable? Did you keep a little back 'just in case'? And when Bertram started his little extortion business, did little bro come crying to you again so that you were glad you still had some poison left?"

"This is utter nonsense," says Goody. "Why on earth would I do that?"

"The eternal motive: love. Firstly, you loved your brother and realised that whatever evidence Bertram had would ensure a custodial sentence for Jack. You knew he couldn't take that. Months or even years in prison would break him and you'd do anything to prevent it. Secondly, you were in love with Mr Manston, weren't you?"

Everyone but Greaty knows that's true. We've often giggled behind her back when she's making googoo eyes at him. Goody's blushing and denying it, of course, and Greaty's looking rather outraged.

"The thought of Mr Manston surrounded by convicts in prison, all his talent wasting away, was too much to bear. Every day, you put up with all the drudgery of your job just to be close to this man, don't you? You hope that one day he'll see how indispensable you are."

That's exactly what I've said about her! She hopes against hope that the fog will lift from his eyes and he'll suddenly see her as the foglight of his life! Mind you, it's not going to happen – Greaty will go on taking what he can without giving her what she desperately wants. I can see him now, looking askance at her, as if he finds all this rather disagreeable.

"Thirdly," continues Grace, ignoring Goody's protestations , "you loved your only friend, Titania, and the thought of her going away with such a horrible man as Bertram tormented you. With Bertram out of the way, Titania would return to the village and take comfort from you, her best mate. She might even move in with you, sealing your importance in her life."

"I've never heard such nonsense. No-one in their right mind would kill for such flimsy reasons – none of which are true anyway. And may I remind you that I have a water-tight alibi? I was at the building site at 4 and it takes me nearly 25 minutes to walk home from there. Titty phoned me at exactly 4.23 – I'd just got home - and we talked for ten minutes. I then had to eat something and change – and anyone who saw me can confirm that I wasn't wearing the same clothes for the evening meeting that I'd been wearing all day. I phoned Greaty at ten past five, and it takes me twenty minutes to walk to his house. He's already told you that I arrived at 5.30. Are you really suggesting that between 4.33 and 5.10, I managed to walk to the theatre – which usually takes me 20minutes – then doctor the toilet door, scatter the bees and wait for Bertram to arrive before poisoning him, replacing the epipen and walking the 15 minute journey to Greaty's? Really? Really? I'm not Superwoman. Surely everyone can see that that just isn't possible?"

Well, she's right, isn't she? No-one could possibly do all that in the time she had. There's a very angry murmur starting up, egged on by an outraged Jack.

"Even if you 'ad a car," he shouts, "you couldn't do it. And not only does Goody not 'ave a car, she can't drive. She walks everywhere unless someone gives her a lift. You haven't done your 'omework and you're accusing an innocent woman of a dreadful crime."

Greaty joins in with "My solicitor will be hearing from me pronto. This is very badly done, Grace."

Tom is watching Grace and Ben very thoughtfully, and he's not joining the rest of us in our outrage. This is making me pause. My Tom is Mr Logical and if he's wondering whether Grace's thesis stands up to scrutiny, then I am too. Grace allows everyone to let off steam before getting Ben to call us to order again. I notice she's still smiling and I think she may have something else up her sleeve.

"You were very precise in telling us the times of your phone calls, which is the beauty of the mobile phone, of course. So there's no dispute whatsoever about those timings," Grace continues blandly.

"Exactly," says Jack triumphantly.

"It's funny, isn't it, how we always assume that calls are made from home. However, you could have made those calls from anywhere, as the word 'mobile' suggests. Now, you were certainly on foot when you went to the building site, and therefore also when you returned from it. So I'm prepared to believe that you spoke to Titania from your home at about 4.30. But your call to Mr Greatorex at 5.10 need not have been from your house."

"The timing still can't be made to work," reasons Greaty. "Without a car, Goody couldn't possibly have covered all the ground necessary and have time to do the dastardly deed with all its ramifications."

"I do not dispute Goody's lack of a car, Mr Greatorex. However, I'm not suggesting that she covered the ground on foot."

I'm puzzled; we're all puzzled. Our little brows are full of furrows. I glance at Tom again, and he's nodding his head. Grace sees him and gives him one of her resplendent smiles. She's obviously glad to see that someone has made the same leap that she has.

Jack is looking justified and mutters that women may be angels but they don't have wings to fly round the town.

Grace is unperturbed and goes on: "I suggest that you got home at 4.33 and got yourself changed ready for the evening, which frankly wouldn't have taken very long. Then you headed up to the theatre and made your preparations, waiting for Bertram to arrive. The pin on the doorknob worked a treat and Bertram panicked that he'd been stung by a bee when he saw the dead ones on the floor, whereupon you produced the poisoned epipen and offered to inject him to save the time it would have taken him to get his own out of his pocket. It would all have happened so fast that he didn't have time to question the logic of your being there with an epipen in your hand. He trusted you implicitly so it wouldn't have occurred to him to doubt your goodwill. Then as he lay dying you took his pristine epi and put it into the First Aid box before sticking the letter for Tony onto the mirror so that it would be found later that evening. Unfortunately, you forgot to remove the pin from the doorknob, which was your only error. You had to do that later in the evening, after Jane had also scratched her hand. That compounded your mistake, because you only had time to throw it on the corridor floor, where I later found it. Then you made sure Bertram was dead and made your way back home to pick up the milk and biscuits before going on to meet Mr Greatorex and Jane at 5.30."

"Aren't you listening, you silly cow?" shouts Jack. "It would take too long for her to do all that walking!"

"Absolutely," says Grace calmly. "But you didn't walk, did you, Goody? Your experience as a sprint cyclist came in handy, didn't it? All that racing when your team won cups?"

"What? I haven't cycled for years. I gave up because my knees were suffering. I don't even know if I kept my bike," splutters Goody.

"Oh, you did, my dear, you certainly did. While searching your garage we found your old bicycle," purrs Ben.

"I'd forgotten all about it," says Goody. "I haven't touched it for yonks."

"Another lie, Goody. The bicycle had been well oiled, the tyres were nicely plump and it was in perfect condition for riding. The fact that you'd thrown it to the back of your garage necessitated a careful search, but we found it with no real trouble. Your journeys weren't carried out on foot but on a racing bike ridden by an experienced competitive cyclist."

"Anybody could have refurbished my bike without my knowledge. For all I know, the village kids could have used it every day while I was at work and I'd never have known. It's that sort of village. We don't lock doors around here, and although my garage is just used as a store, I never lock it. Everything you say is mere fantasy and no Court would pay it any heed. Circumstantial, I think that's the word," Goody asserts, though I can see she's sweating a bit.

"Then it's fortunate that you left handy little fingerprints behind, isn't it? On the bike – and elsewhere," says Ben.

"What? What do you mean? That's impossible. Or if you mean on the loo door or something, then of course that's because I took Jane to the toilet to show her where it was. I could have touched anything then and it wouldn't prove a thing."

Grace smiles like the cat that got the creep and we all know there's another nail about to be knocked in Goody's coffee.

"Did you know that sticky tape is a wonderful harbourer of fingerprints?" asks Grace. "That little mistake you made when you forgot to remove the drawing pin from the doorknob will cost you dear. There's a perfect match on the sticky surface."

Goody's mouth drops open but she hasn't finished fighting yet. I have to admire her perseverance.

"That could have been dropped in the corridor days before. I often stick things on the notice board, so it's not surprising that my prints would be there. This is still utterly preposterous and as far-fetched as the script for our panto."

"Ah, but Jane's blood was there, too, which narrows it down to her scratching her hand on the handle. There was no other way her blood could have been deposited on the drawing pin."

"You're nicked, Sunshine," says Ben smugly.

Chapter 19

The village hasn't been the same since the arrest. It's as if there's been a major earth tremor that has shaken everything up. The effects have been felt through the whole community. No doubt there will be further prosecutions arising out of the information gleaned by Bertram and hidden in his room. There are all sorts of whispers going around. It's certainly affecting our panto group, I can tell you.

Greaty is hurrying his prestige housing development along as fast as he can (and we can't help wondering if he's doing that to get it built before he's charged with something). There's a lot of scepticism in the village about buying one of his houses now, with people wondering about his honesty. Is he the sort to cut corners and use inferior quality materials just to make a bigger profit? What will people find if they dig up the garden? So apparently he's going to use an outside estate agent and concentrate on the DFLs (that's the Down From Londoners, in case you don't know the jargon). He's so busy and stressed that he's cancelled the panto, not just postponed it. Nobody's surprised. In fact, we're all rather relieved.

Jack's working his socks off for Greaty. Those two are an unlikely pairing but they're shoulder to shoulder now. Maybe it's a case of Honour Among Thieves, but I think it's more about watching each other's moves and keeping their story straight. We don't know quite what evidence Bertram had or whether it would stand up in court after the Enquiry had already found nothing against Greaty or Jack. They must be walking on eggshells, but at least they're walking together. Jack is being very good about visiting Goody in the nick while she's waiting for her trial. Now she's not around to look after him, he's standing on his own feet much more. It's strange that a tragedy can sometimes bring out the better side of people. He's always been a chancer who would take risks because big sis was there to pick up the bits when things went wrong. This might be the making of him – as long as he can avoid prison himself.

Mimi's presenting a cheerful face to the world and being as nice as pike to her clients – but I notice she doesn't wear that amber necklace any more. It must be a difficult line to walk sometimes if you have grateful clients who want to show their appreciation of your care of them. A box of choccies, a bunch of flowers – that's all right, surely. But a more expensive gift? A tenner for your birthday – "Get something nice for yourself, darling"? A shy promise of something in the will? You see what I mean. Where does it become wrong? If you should say No to everything, wouldn't it be hurtful and stupid to say No to a bunch of daffodils? Anyway, Mimi is being ultra careful right now.

The sale of Leela's shop may fall through, unsurprisingly. Rumours of asbestos got around and the buyer has stepped back a few paces. Leela is still insisting that her basement is fine, but when the prospective buyer asked her to provide proof, she insisted that it was up to the buyer's surveyor to prove otherwise. That didn't go down well. In the hopes of coming to an eventual compromise, Leela's old man is paying for a survey of Wendy's basement. That may sound illogical, but you'll remember that Bertram said there was similar asbestos in her shop, screwing some extra money out of innocent little Wendy. Doing a survey on Wendy's basement will be a doddle, whereas taking down the new cladding in Leela's to get at the original wall underneath would be really expensive. In the meantime, Leela is still plungeing her hands into cold water every day and moaning about her rheumatism.

Wendy carries on in her fey way (I nearly wrote Faye Wray there!) She's still knitting up a storm and giving crochet lessons to a group of youngsters who think it's trendy. She's none too bright – in fact, she's a picnic short of a picnic – but she's an absolute whizz with her hands. She can knit patterns that would send me into conniptions and she can fashion a Cinderella ballgown out of crepe paper and tinsel in the twinkling of a pie. I really hope the asbestos scare was a scam from Bertram and not a reality. All Wendy wants is a dust-free environment for her beloved fabrics and she deserves to have one.

Robbie is moving on to a different brewery and is leaving the village as soon as a replacement is hired for the pub here. His wife, Alice, can be heard giving him grief every night after the pub closes – and she's the one who keeps the books nowadays. A wise move. I expect she'll cover any discrepancies here and keep a firmer hand on the tiller in their next pub. I'll be sorry to lose Alice from the village, and Robbie was always a good laugh at rehearsals, but needs must when the Devil dives.

Titania has gone back to live with her parents in Gloucestershire. They didn't know that she and Tony weren't married so they're really thankful now that she's free of him. Apparently, they never liked him but she wouldn't listen to them. Well, what girl does listen to her mum and dad when lerv is concerned? Tony is still a miserable sod and he seems to be drinking more of his stock than selling it. I can't see the offy surviving long. Tony's not going to find a new mate here in the village, not now we know about his cruelty to Titty, so hopefully he'll be on his way.

The only people to have emerged unscathed are those who had nothing to hide in the first place. So Bunty can breathe a sigh of relief because Bertram lied to her about having a pill pack with the wrong dose printed on it. I think she might finally retire. Chris and Freddy's alibi was faultless and they weren't even called in to the Startling Dénouement meeting. We all wondered about the CX? in Bertram's notebook, and I'm hoping that if Chris was trying to hide his sexuality that he'll have the courage to come out now. Nobody gives a toss (if you'll pardon the expression) about such things nowadays.

Actually, Freddy is surprising us all. He's stepping forward to take on the Summer production, just in case Greaty is elsewhere. It turns out that he knows much more about theatre than we thought. We're so used to talking about him as Camp Freddy (as opposed to Camp David in America) and he's so used to playing up to that image just for the fun of it, that his knowledge of plays has been overlooked. He's a walking play list! Where we were all giving up the idea of a production because a) perhaps no Greaty and b) perhaps no Jack to do the construction, Freddy was beavering away at finding a play that wouldn't need a set. He's come up with 'Waiting for Godot'. I've never heard of it but Tom says it's a classic. Freddy says it can be done with just a tree on stage. We all laughed at that idea at first, but he says it will be extra funny having a single tree in a bucket as the only scenery, with just black curtains at the back and sides of the stage. He's even got the local Garden Centre to donate the tree! He's persuaded them that at the end of the performances, they can have the tree back and auction it off as "The Godot Tree – as seen on stage". He reckons they'll get more money for it than it was originally worth. Brilliant idea, say I. What's more, he's going to cast it with all women! Usually, it's all men, but our little am dram society has the same problems that all of them do, that there are more women than men in the group. He's really being avant garde and we all love it.

And what of me and Tom? We're having a whale of a time, thank you. All the gossip gets filtered through here along with the coffee. My mince pies have been a runaway success this Christmas. We make our own mincemeat the year before and let it soak in brandy for a whole year. Tom thinks his hand must have slipped last year when he was adding the Courvoisier, so this year's batch is extra delicious. Did I tell you my pastry secrets? I use frozen filo and puff but I make my own shortcrust. I add a little demerara castor sugar to the mix and I always use the best free range egg yolks. I sprinkle a little demerara castor sugar on top, which gives a slight crunch on top of the melt-in-the-mouth pastry (and if customers want theirs warmed up, the sugar on top begins melting into a toffee-flavoured crispness). Tom and I make them fresh every day, so why don't you make a trip to Middle Pidding and try one?

Printed in Great Britain
by Amazon

60219352R00117